TWO STOLEN MEN

A Park Pals Mystery
Book 4

Dwain Cassady

LAP CAT
PUBLISHING

TWO

STOLEN

MEN

CHAPTER 1

Shivering, shaking, and cold, he awoke in darkness. He was lying on something hard, head pounding. Moving to sit up, dizziness attacked, so he lay back down and curled into a ball, trying to gain as much warmth as he could.

Why am I so cold? I must have tripped and hit my head on something. Did someone steal my coat?

He felt and found the coat was still in place, even zipped. He tried to remember what had happened, but his mind seemed incapable of recall. *Am I dreaming? I hope I wake up before I freeze to death.*

The thought occurred to him to pinch himself as they do in movies. *I felt that, so I must be awake. I've got to get someplace warmer. I didn't think it was supposed to be this cold tonight. … Was that a memory? My head's killin' me.*

He tried sitting up again. The dizziness returned, but being more awake, he pushed on. *That's progress. Let's see what happens when I stand up.*

He got to his feet, and his hand found purchase on something cold and hard. The darkness span until he retched and puked on the floor. *I guess I'd better lie back down.*

He moved away from the puke and hit something. It felt like a shelf. He knelt down and felt around on the floor to make sure he was clear of the vomit. *I must have gone blind when I hit my head.*

Muffled voices filtered through the confusion. He looked in the direction from which they came but saw only blackness.

"Help!" he yelled.

The voices sounded closer, then a searing light erased the thought that he had gone blind.

CHAPTER 2

The park pals gathered at Laurel Park on a beautiful Monday morning. It was the last week in October, and the maples were showing off their colors.

"I hope the sun is hitting the maples by the time we're back. That would make a wondrous photo. Hmm, I wonder if I could catch the sunrise through the leaves," Katía mused as she brushed back her black locks that were especially wild today.

Luna hopped out of her car, squealing with excitement. "I can't believe the wedding is less than two weeks away! I hope the day is as pretty as this one!" She ran and hugged Katía, then moved to Fitz. He stiffened, patted her back with one hand, then pulled out a few M&Ms.

"Really, Fitz?" Katía scolded.

He shrugged his shoulders. "I'm working on it." He tugged his long, scraggly, graying beard and forced himself not to reach for more M&Ms.

"I'll have to admit you've come a long way. I'd better not see you going for the M&Ms after hugging me, though," Katía added.

"Yes, ma'am."

"Is there anything else we need to do to get ready for the wedding?" Luna asked.

Katía opened her phone to the checklist she had created. "My final dress fitting is this afternoon. Fitz's tux is ready to be picked up. The food will be delivered to the park. As far as I can tell, it's all ready."

"You did remember to line up a preacher, right?" Zee asked. "If not, I'll be happy to do one of those online ordinations right quick." He bent his long, lanky self down to rub his arthritic knee.

"Yep. Brian, my good friend from seminary, is flying in on Thursday. I even have picking him up at the airport on the calendar." Katía grinned.

"You're so organized," Ben added as Snickers tugged at her leash. "Snickers says it's time to get going." Ben, in his early seventies and sporting a neatly-trimmed, salt-and-pepper beard, bent to pat his labradoodle.

Fitz had his ginger cat, Buffett, harnessed up. Buffett enjoyed walking with the park pals, particularly with Snickers and with Zee's little dog, King. The group of five people and three pets set off for the trail that looped the park. When they were halfway around the trail, Luna, a retired teacher, stopped. "I just realized I never asked about the proposal.

How'd he do it?" She took Katía by the arm and hustled to catch up with Fitz, Ben, and Zee.

Katía grinned. "Perfect timing. He asked me out for a picnic here at the park. We sat on that bench near the lake," she pointed. "We ate fried chicken and watched the boats go by. Before I realized what was happening, he got down on a knee and asked me to marry him. I jumped up so fast I knocked my Coke over. I couldn't get yes out quickly enough."

"You're speedy," Zee quipped, poking Fitz in the shoulder.

"There was no doubt I wanted to marry him from the moment being trapped in that cave unlocked the awareness of my feelings for him," Katía said with a shudder, remembering her time of being hogtied in what the Inmansons had called, "the dying cave."

"I just wonder how you're gonna survive bein' cooped up in a house," Zee mused, talking to Fitz who, like Zee, lived in his car.

"I'll be with Katía. I don't see it being a problem," Fitz answered.

"Have you decided whether to have the ceremony by the lake or in front of the maple trees yet?" Ben asked.

"We're still bouncing back and forth on that one. Since I noticed the maple trees are losing their leaves at the tops, I'd prefer the lake. How about you, Fitz?"

"I'm happy with the lake," he replied, trying to sneak another bite of M&Ms without her seeing him.

"I saw that," Katía said.

"Give him a break," Luna replied. "It's perfectly normal to be nervous before a wedding."

"Amen," Ben and Zee echoed.

As they continued along the trail, a portly man with a small black, gray, and white dog approached in the distance. His brown hair was pressed as neatly as his clothes.

"Be nice, Snickers," Ben said.

"I wonder who that is," Zee added.

When the man was close enough to make out his features, Katía whispered, "It's Councilman Johnston. He's a member of my church."

The dogs gathered together to sniff each other, and Buffett sat nearby. Katía said, "Good morning, Councilman. What brings you to the park this glorious morning?"

"I've heard you talk about how nice it is, so I thought I'd try it myself. Hi, Fitz." He extended his hand to Ben. "Let me introduce myself. I'm Winslow Johnston, and this is Rip."

"It's nice to meet you. Ben Blessing, and the nosey dog is Snickers." Snickers was sniffing Winslow to see if he had any dog treats.

Taking a step back from Snickers, Winslow introduced himself to Zee and Luna.

After the introductions, Katía said, "I heard about the vote last night, and I'm torn. I'm sorry you lost your bid for the property, but I have to admit I'm happy the shelter project can move forward. Are you OK with the vote?"

Winslow put his free hand to his chin, then lowered it. "I have to admit I'm disappointed. I need that property to expand my restaurant business. If the shelter fails to materialize, I'll try again. I must get going so I can get to the office. It was certainly nice to meet all of you. Have a good day. Come on, Rip."

As he walked on down the trail, Luna said, "The shelter was approved? That's huge! Congratulations!"

"It passed four to two. Our friend, Winslow, was one of the two who voted against it," Katía replied. "He wanted the property to build another restaurant, as you gathered. I'm sure he's more upset than he let on. I'm afraid there'll be tension in the church for a while."

"Y'all are one of the sponsorin' churches, too," Zee added. "When it's up and runnin', I might just hang out there some."

"You should. We're planning to have a space where people can get in out of the weather, use computers, and do laundry," Katía added.

"Showers for us residentially-challenged folks would be nice, too," Zee grinned.

"They're planning to have those," Fitz added.

"Let's get back to the wedding," Luna said. "I can pick your dress up when it's ready. Are you sure you don't want any flowers?"

"I'm sure. We're trying to keep this as simple as possible. I'll have to try on the dress one more time when I pick it up, though," Katía answered.

"Well, I think the lake is prettier than flowers, anyway," Ben added.

"We have to have at least two pots of flowers for you to stand between. I'll order them myself," Luna insisted.

After finishing the walk around the trail, Katía went home, dressed, and headed for the church. When she arrived, she noticed that the side door leading to her office was open. *That's odd.* Seeing no other cars in the parking lot, she proceeded with caution, her right hand in her purse and gripping the pistol she always carried. *Just in case.*

She entered the door and scanned the hallway. *Nothing seems amiss.* Working her way along the hallway, she checked each room. Nothing was out of order. Two thoughts crashed in her mind. *Maybe wind just blew the door open.* And *oh, no! The offering!*

Rushing into the sanctuary, she saw the box with its lid on the floor. The congregation had been collecting money to support the new shelter for unhoused people. Congregants placed their donations into a locked box, and they planned to open the box the Sunday before Thanksgiving to see how much they had collected.

Both hands went to her cheeks as she gasped. The box was empty.

CHAPTER 3

Standing in front of the empty offering box that was meant to collect money for the shelter, Katía shivered. She wasn't sure if it was rage or anguish. *I wonder how much money we lost. What do I do now?*

Shocked by her discovery, it took Katía a few moments to regain sense enough to call 911 to report the robbery. As soon as she hung up, she called Fitz. "Someone broke into the church and stole our shelter offering!"

"What?" Fitz said, pausing.

Katía sensed he was trying to process the idea of someone robbing a church. "Someone stole the money we had collected for the new shelter," she repeated.

"I'm on my way over."

"Weren't you going to pick up your tuxedo?"

"Yeah, but that can wait."

Katía disconnected the call and wrapped her arms around herself. *I'm glad he's coming. ... I'd better take some pictures of the scene.* She snapped a few photos, then went to her office to wait. She started to pull up the sermon ideas she had begun for Sunday but decided it would be pointless. *I'll never be able to concentrate.*

After about ten minutes, which had seemed like an eternity, she heard a car pull up. *That must be the police.* She went out to find a deputy sitting in the car and writing. When the door opened, she was glad to see a familiar face. "Hey, Deputy James. I'm glad you came."

"Please, call me Diann. I feel like we know each other too well for formalities. Now tell me what happened," the fit-looking brunette deputy said.

Katía went through her discovery of the open door and the broken offering box as she led Diann into the church to show her the scene.

Katía noticed Diann looking up and down as she walked toward the sanctuary.

"I don't see any security cameras," Diann said.

"No, we don't have any. We've talked about installing them but haven't yet."

While Diann was taking photographs, Katía heard another car pull up. "That's probably Fitz."

"Why would Fitz be showing up?" Diann asked.

"I called him. He's my fiancé."

"You're marrying Fitz Fitzgerald? May the Lord give you strength," Diann chuckled.

Fitz hurried into the sanctuary and embraced Katía. "Are you OK?"

"I'm a little shaken but fine other than that."

Diann cleared her throat. "How much was stolen?"

"Actually, I don't know. We decided to collect the money but wait until the Sunday before Thanksgiving to open the box and count it," Katía replied.

"When was the last time you saw the offering box intact?"

Katía thought back to yesterday. "Did I go into the sanctuary when I stopped in on the youth meeting? … I did because I had left my Bible on the pulpit. I remember looking at the box and wondering how much was in it, but I resisted the temptation to unlock it. That was about five-thirty yesterday afternoon."

Diann wrote in her little notebook. "Did you publicize the offering in the community or just at church?"

"Just at church," Katía answered.

Fitz was bent over, looking at the lock.

"Don't touch anything. We'll need to dust for prints," Diann warned.

"I'm not going to touch anything," Fitz huffed, "but I don't think you'll get any prints. It looks like it's been wiped."

Diann looked closely at the lock and saw the telltale signs of smudges running in one direction on the steel. "Somebody didn't want to get caught."

She straightened up. "If only your congregation knew about the money, I'm afraid your members and their associates are the most likely suspects."

"I don't believe anyone in the congregation would have done this," Katía said.

"People do talk, though. I'm going to need you to make a list of church folks and their family members who have drug issues, mental health issues, or financial woes. The family members, or even their friends, could have learned of the offering and decided they needed it more than the church. The sooner you can get that list to me, the better."

"The doorknob's been wiped, too," Fitz added.

"Do you want to take over the investigation?" Diann scoffed.

Fitz held up his hands. "Just trying to be helpful."

Diann held out a card to Katía. "Text or email me the list you come up with, please."

"I'll go over our membership list first thing and get that to you."

Diann left Fitz and Katía in the sanctuary.

"She's right," Fitz said. "I didn't see any signs of forced entry at the door, so whoever did this either has a key or knows how to pick a lock."

"Or we forgot to lock it yesterday evening."

"That opens another possibility. The door could have been left unlocked in preparation for the theft."

"I don't think anyone who was here yesterday evening would do such a thing." Katía put her hands on her hips. "Do I clean this up or leave it here in case they want to have another look?"

"Let's leave it and get to work on identifying suspects," Fitz said.

Sadness hit as Katía stared at the wrecked box. The wood surrounding the lock had been sawed. Sawdust littered the floor. "Jack put a lot of work into making that box. … We needed that money for the shelter. How could anyone bring themselves to steal it?"

She wiped a falling tear, and Fitz took her in his arms. "It was just money. I'm grateful no one was hurt," he said.

Katía took a deep breath. "I'll put on some coffee. Check to see if Buffett wants to help."

"Yeah, I'll get him."

Katía noticed Fitz pulling out M&Ms as he walked out the door. She smiled. *At least I'll always know when you're stressed about something.*

With coffee brewing, she and Fitz sat down in the office. Buffett hopped onto her desk and rubbed against Katía's arm. "Thanks, Buffett," she said as she opened the file with the list of members. "I'm just going to read through the list and see if it jogs my memory."

Fitz pulled over a legal pad. "I'll write while you talk."

Katía read through the list in alphabetical order, stopping occasionally to mention people whose family members fit the categories Diann had listed. When she was in the Ds, she looked at Fitz. "I still find it hard to believe it could have been anyone associated with the church."

"How else would they have known the money was here? Since you didn't find anything else missing, that had to be what they were after."

"What if it was just a druggie who broke in hoping to find money and discovered the box?"

Fitz tugged at his beard. "If that were the case, why would they have brought a saw?"

Katía rested her head in her hands and puzzled. "That does make it seem like they knew about the offering, doesn't it?"

With the aroma of coffee scenting the room, Fitz said, "I believe the coffee's done." He poured two mugs. Buffett raised his head from where he'd gone to sleep on the desk, looking expectantly at Fitz. "You expect coffee, too? OK, here's some cat coffee." He pulled out a few treats and laid them on the desk, rubbing Buffett's back as he gobbled them down.

"Back to it," Katía said and resumed working through the list of members. She pressed on till she came to the Js. "Winslow Johnston and his wife Stacey. You met him at the park today. He's a work in progress for sure. The man has been pressing the city council to round up and remove the unhoused population for months. So far, no one else has supported him. I don't see how he can think that way and still come to church every Sunday. He's certainly not listening when I'm preaching," she laughed before continuing down the list.

When they had finished, Katía had identified thirteen potential suspects. She texted the list to Diann. "I have a meeting with the shelter committee at ten-thirty. I'd better get going. Do you and Buffett want to hang out at the house?"

"I need to go get that tux. … Would you mind if I stored it at your house, though? I don't think it'll fare too well in the car."

"You mean our house. Of course you can hang it there, silly." She rounded the desk and gave him a hug and a kiss. "Thanks for staying with me this morning. It helped me get through the shock."

"Anytime," Fitz smiled.

Still hugging Fitz, Katía raised her watch so she could see it over his shoulder. "Oh, no! I'm going to be late! Lock up, will you?" She grabbed her purse and rushed out the door.

CHAPTER 4

atía rushed into the conference room at First Baptist Church, out of breath from hurrying. Jim Hamilton, the church's sandy-haired, blue-eyed pastor, strode over to greet her.

"It's so good to see you, Katía. We're just about to get started. You see the coffee and tea station." He gestured.

"Thanks," she replied. "I'll take another cup of coffee. This has been a rough morning." Katía noticed the eyes of the other five ministers were trained on her. "Someone broke into our church last night and stole the offering we were collecting for the shelter project."

She sensed the shock wave that went through the group, and each one expressed their concern or anger.

"I'm glad no one was hurt," Jim said. "At least we have good news this morning. Let's focus on that. With the council voting to let us buy the property and develop the shelter, we have lots of planning to do!"

Sitting around the elegant walnut conference table, Jim led them in a prayer before opening the discussion. "I've put together a list of decisions I think we need to make in order to move forward. Number one, we need to assess whether we can use the old motel with renovations or do we need to tear it down and start fresh."

"I don't see the current facility fitting our vision. I think it's going to have to come down," Roger O'Brien, pastor of Prince of Peace Presbyterian church said.

"Before we throw the baby out with the bathwater, I think we need to get estimates of renovation possibilities versus building something new. We need to know the costs of our options," Katía added.

"But how much would it cost to do that kind of study?" Charis Stanton, pastor of Vine and Branches Lutheran church asked as she pushed her auburn hair behind an ear. "We have to be good stewards of our limited resources."

Alister Bates, pastor of St. Peter Baptist Church, set his coffee mug down and put his fingertips together. "We also have to have faith that the Lord will provide. I say we get a contractor out of one of our churches to have a look and give us some rough estimates."

"That's a good idea," Jim said. "And that brings us to our next item: Exactly what do we want to include and how shall we set up the new facility? What will the client rooms look like, how will the common areas be arranged, what other spaces do we need?"

"To keep from getting our wagon ahead of the horse, I think we need to nail down the specifics before deciding on renovation versus building," Father Ansel Anderson, priest of St. Mark's Catholic church, said.

Catrina Sanchéz, pastor of Palabra de Vida church, added, "Let's make that our homework. Before the next meeting, everyone make a list of ideas for how they would like the facility to be set up, and we can pool our thoughts."

"That's positively perfect," Bill Olster, pastor of First United Methodist Church, added. "I've already started on my list."

"This is so exciting!" Katía said, rubbing her hands together. "I'm happy we get to move forward with our plans."

* * * * *

"Oh, me, Buffett," Fitz said, sitting in the driveway at Katía's house. He popped a few M&Ms into his mouth. "I've never been inside without her being there. This is strange."

"Meow."

"Good idea. I think you should come with me."

Getting out, he harnessed up Buffett, picked up the tux, then realized he'd left the code for the front door in the console between the front seats. "Hang on a minute." He folded the tux over his arm and leaned in to get the slip of paper on which he had written the code. Realizing the tux would drag the ground, he hung it back up, got the paper, and retrieved the tux. Finally, he headed for the door.

Buffett sniffed around while Fitz had one more round of M&Ms before punching in the code for the electric lock. Snow and Cotton, Katía's two long-haired white cats, eyed him from the den, poised to dash under the couch if necessary.

"Be nice," Fitz said to Buffett, who strode in, tail high, as if he were king of the castle.

Fitz stood still. Like a stormy sea, emotions roiled. "We're going to be living here … soon." The words rang hollow as his soul resisted the thought of being confined to four walls.

Cotton and Snow, having gotten to know Fitz and Buffett on their previous visits, strolled over to greet Buffett.

Fitz stood still, listening to the sounds of the house: a clock ticking, the refrigerator running. *It sounds friendly.* The front door opened into a small living room, followed by the kitchen, den, and a hallway leading to the three bedrooms and two bathrooms.

Feet rooted to the ground, Fitz ate more M&Ms, tugged on his beard, and said in a whisper, "We're going to live here. I don't know if I can do this." He pried his feet loose and turned back toward the door. With his hand reaching for the doorknob, he stopped. *I can't do this either.*

Buffett was taking a bath, Cotton and Snow having wandered back to the den. "I see you're making yourself at home."

"Meow."

"I guess I need to figure out how to do that, too." More M&Ms, then he turned back around. "I'm glad Katía didn't see me nearly leave." He took a deep breath, dropped Buffett's leash, and walked through the living room and down the hall.

Passing the bathroom, he smiled. "No more hunting for toilets." Conflicted, he stopped. The master bedroom was to his left and another to his right. He turned into the room on the right. *I don't think I should put the tux in her closet.* Buffett moved along on silent cat feet, dragging the leash.

"Sorry, Buffett. I should have taken that off." Fitz scolded himself for his absent-mindedness. He hung up the tuxedo, unhooked the leash, then stood at the doorway of the master bedroom. "Everything's neat and tidy. Organized." He didn't go in.

"Now what, Buffett?"

"Meow." Buffett trotted off to the kitchen in search of food.

"Is that all you think about?" Fitz followed him and found him eating dry food from a bowl. He noticed Katía's bowl and coffee mug in the sink. "I'm going to wash these while you eat."

With the dishes washed, Fitz said, "I think we'd better go, don't you?"

Buffett's ears went back in annoyance. Fitz walked out of the kitchen and noticed the TV. *How long has it been since I watched TV?* Like a moth drawn to light, he found himself in the den holding the remote. Snow or Cotton, whom he had not yet learned to tell apart, sat on one end of the couch, so he sat on the opposite end.

"Do you mind if I sit here?" he asked the cat. She eyed him warily but didn't jump down. "Thanks, Snow … or are you Cotton?" Katía had explained which one wore the black collar with pink stars and which wore the pink collar with black stars, but it hadn't stuck in Fitz's memory yet. He did remember they were sisters.

He turned on the TV, and the local news came on. They were talking about a break-in at a local restaurant.

"Allegedly, an unhoused man broke into The Oasis restaurant in Gainesville and attempted a robbery. Authorities report that the man was found in the kitchen's refrigerator room, where he appeared to have tripped and hit his head, knocking himself unconscious.

"The restaurant is owned by Winslow Johnston, a city councilman." The camera turned to Johnston. "Mr. Johnston, can you tell us any more about what happened?"

"I arrived at the restaurant this morning at nine o'clock. One of the first things I do is check the supplies needed for the day. When I opened the refrigerator door, I found a man lying there unconscious with money from the safe scattered around him.

"I want the city to know that there has been a rash of break-ins by the homeless population recently, including my own church. Last night, a homeless person broke into St. Luke United Methodist Church and stole thirty-six hundred dollars from an offering box. The money was being collected for the new homeless shelter that area churches are planning to build.

"This crime spree has to stop, and it won't end until we rid the city of this nuisance population. I believe it is time for us to empower the police to arrest these vagrants and put them in jail. We might even consider calling out the National Guard. I plan to make these proposals at our council meeting tomorrow evening."

Fitz's anger flamed, and he turned off the TV. "How dare you blame the church break-in on a residentially-challenged person! It could have just as easily been you!" he yelled at the TV.

The white cat jumped off the couch at his outburst.

CHAPTER 5

Fitz loaded Buffett into his old Highlander and drove toward town to meet Katía for lunch. Being fifteen minutes early, he found a parking space on the square and waited.

"I miss Katía when she's working," Fitz confided to his ever-faithful cat.

"Meow."

"You, too, huh?"

"Meow.

Buffett rubbed Fitz on the chin before settling back onto his lap. Fitz petted the cat as he stewed over the councilman's accusations about the unhoused population. *I don't see how people can be so bigoted. And he's supposed to represent all the people. Ugh. I hope he gets voted out next time.*

Fitz checked his watch. "I'm going on in to get us a table."

"Meow."

"Yes, I'll save a bite for you."

Walking into the Collegiate Grill, Fitz spotted a table in the back. Rather than getting into the order line, he went on and sat down, watching for Katía.

His heart quickened when he saw her at the door, and he hurried to the front to meet her.

"Did you miss me terribly?" she asked.

"How did you know?"

"I can see it in your eyes. It also looks like you're mad about something."

Fitz looked into her eyes. "How do you do that?"

"Do what?"

"Read me like that."

"I'll never tell," she grinned. "It's such a gorgeous day, let's eat outside on the square. You can let Buffett out of the car for a bit."

"Sounds good to me."

"Then you can tell me what's bugging you."

Fitz left Katía sitting on a bench with their meals while he harnessed Buffett and tied his leash to the bench. They tucked into their burgers, and after a few bites, Katía asked, "So what's got you angry? I hope it's not something I did."

"It's nothing you did."

"Well, what is it then?"

Fitz realized it would be easier to talk about it than to try steering Katía onto another topic. "I turned on the TV while I was at your house."

"Our house. I'm proud of you! But that shouldn't make you mad."

"That councilman was on the news."

"… And that made you mad?" Katía put down her burger and picked up a French fry.

"He was griping about residentially-challenged folks, saying we should all be arrested." Fitz's face contorted with anger. "He even said it was one of us who broke into the church!"

"Yeah, he's not my favorite parishioner. He can be petty, but how did he make the leap to its being a residentially-challenged person who broke into the church? So far, we have no idea who did it."

Fitz swallowed a drink of Coke. "He went on to say that he plans to introduce an ordinance to have the police arrest all unhoused people in the city."

"That's terrible."

Fitz clenched his fist. "He's threatening to call in the National Guard to round us up."

"That's not even legal. He can't do that. I understand you're angry about this, and we need to channel that anger into preventing this from happening."

"Have you never heard the saying, 'You can't fight city hall?' Well, that's especially true for people like us. No one's going to listen to a bunch of unhoused people. They'll side with that goat of a councilman."

"I'd listen to you, and I'm someone."

Fitz reached out and took her hand. "Yeah, but you're about to marry me."

Katía smiled, leaned over and kissed him, then said, "I'd listen to you even if I weren't in love with you. There are plenty of people who care about the plight of folks without homes. That's why the city is coming together to build a new shelter, and we're going to get as many of the church folks as we can to be at that meeting to oppose his proposal. Did he say when it was?"

"Tomorrow evening," Fitz growled. He stood up and walked away.

"Hey, where are you going? We need to plan an attack against his proposal," Katía said.

Fitz turned and said, "I'm going to muster the residentially-challenged folks to show up tomorrow night."

"That's a great idea, Fitz, but you can finish lunch first. Buffett might like to come along with you, too."

Fitz's shoulders sagged. "I've been so scatterbrained lately."

"It's called wedding stress. Sit down and let's finish our nice lunch before we get busy mobilizing people for tomorrow's meeting." She patted the bench. "Besides, it's illegal to leave your fiancé without giving her a kiss."

Fitz picked up his burger, sat right next to Katía, and planted a kiss on her lips. "I don't ever want to miss one of those."

Katía took a bite of burger, then started strategizing. "How can you get the unhoused folks to show up? I mean, how can we get them there?"

"Some have cars. Most would have to walk."

"What if we run some church vans to pick them up?"

Fitz grinned. "Did anyone ever tell you you're brilliant?"

"You just did. Where would some good pick-up spots be?

"I'll make you a list of the encampments. First, let me see how much interest I can generate."

"Great. I'll get on the phone and start mobilizing churches. We're going to let him know exactly what this city thinks of his plan. Oh, we need to text the park pals. Oh! I have to get to my dress fitting, too!"

With lunch finished, Fitz was calmer. He untied Buffett's leash and headed to his car while Katía texted the park pals.

Fitz smiled while he unleashed Buffett, who was sitting in the driver's seat. He opened his phone to read the text Katía had sent to the park pals explaining the situation and asking them to get everyone they could to be at the meeting tomorrow evening. He turned off the screen, and Buffett jumped to the passenger seat as he sat down.

Parking on the side of the road near the first encampment, he walked down a path along a creek. Seeing tents up ahead, he called out, "Sarge, I come in peace." Hearing no response, he called again. "Sarge."

A rustling sound preceded the unzipping of a tent door ahead to Fitz's right. A baseball bat appeared, followed by an arm, then a woman with leathery skin and gray hair.

"Hey, Sarge," Fitz said, noticing the recognition in her eyes.

"If it ain't my favorite Fitz. What are you doin' draggin' me out of bed this time of day?"

Fitz realized his mistake. "Sorry, I forgot this is your sleeping time."

"Well, I'm up now. What do you want?"

"Have you heard of the city councilman named Winslow Johnston?"

"Nah. I don't keep up with politics." Sarge rested the head of the bat on the ground.

"He's on a mission to get residentially-challenged folks rounded up and thrown in jail."

"Somebody's always tryin' to get rid of us. Ain't nothin' new."

"It gets worse. He's proposing an ordinance to call for the police to start arresting us. He's even threatening to call in the National Guard. Anyway, I'm trying to get people to show up at the council meeting tomorrow night to protest his ordinance and see if we can get it voted down."

A big grin grew on Sarge's face. "Me and ole Betsy'll be happy to give that councilman a piece of our minds." She smacked the bat into her palm.

"You should probably leave Betsy in the tent," Fitz chuckled. "Could you help spread the word? We need as many people as possible to show up."

"Yeah, I'll tell everybody I see. Did ya hear about Harley?"

"No, what happened?" Fitz asked.

"He didn't come back to his tent last night. Word is they caught him in the fridge at a restaurant. Claim he broke in."

"Yeah, I did hear about that, but I didn't realize it was Harley. The restaurant belongs to the councilman I told you about."

"You sure I can't bring Betsy? I can't believe Harley'd rob a restaurant."

"Somebody broke into my fiancé's church last night, and the good councilman went on TV and claimed it was an unhoused person who did it," Fitz said.

"If I didn't need my beauty sleep, me and Betsy'd go have a talk with that man right now."

"Have you heard any talk about one of us breaking into the church?"

"Nope."

"I hope a little more sleep will calm you down. When you wake up, tell everybody you see about the meeting. It's tomorrow night at seven-thirty."

"Don't worry, I'll get a posse there."

"Thanks, Sarge. There'll be a van here about six-fifty to give folks a ride." Fitz returned to his car and drove to the encampment where his old army pal, Captain, stayed.

"Hey, Fitz!" Captain, AKA Roy Rollins, said, extending his hand as Fitz walked up.

"Hey, Captain. How are you?"

"I've got food in my belly and beautiful weather. Can't get much better'n that. What brings you to my humble abode?"

"Have you heard about Councilman Johnston's plan to have all unhoused folks jailed?"

"Yeah. That man needs to get out of government and stick to the restaurant business." Captain folded his arms.

Fitz continued, "He went on TV today and said he's proposing an ordinance to accomplish his goal at tomorrow's council meeting." Fitz went on to explain the need to get people to show up at the meeting, and Captain promised to pass the word.

"Great," Fitz replied. "We'll have a van here about seven o'clock. I guess you heard about Harley getting arrested."

"Yeah, that's a shame. I guess he got greedy."

"Sarge said she couldn't believe he'd do such a thing."

"It does seem out of character, but do we ever really know another person? Heck, do we ever really know ourselves?"

CHAPTER 6

Luna chatted as the park pals made their usual morning walk along the trail. "You're going to look so beautiful in your wedding dress! I don't believe we could have found a better one!"

"I sure appreciate you going with me to pick it up," Katía replied.

"You got a picture?" Zee asked.

"No, no, no! You can't see her till the wedding," Luna scolded.

"I thought that just applied to Fitz," Zee suggested.

"Good try, Zee," Luna replied.

"How do you think tonight's meeting will go?" Ben asked, prompting Fitz to pop M&Ms into his mouth.

"I believe we're going to have a huge turnout," Katía answered. "I just hope it's enough to convince the council to vote against Winslow's proposal."

"You're not really worried, are you?" Luna asked.

After a pause, Katía said, "Just a little. The consequences of failing are huge."

Fitz clenched his fist. "We can't afford to fail."

Fitz and Buffett arrived at Katía's house at 4:45 Tuesday evening. "I have to have supper cooked so we can leave by six-thirty," he explained to Buffett. "I don't want Katía to have to rush in and try to put food on the table."

Using the keypad, he unlocked the door. Two white faces peeked from the den as Cotton and Snow checked the intruders. "Tonight's a big night. We have to stop an ornery councilman from imprisoning all the residentially-challenged folks in the city."

"Meow."

"I'm going to let you stay here with Cotton and Snow. I don't think they'd let you into the meeting."

"Meow." Buffett rubbed against his legs.

"Of course you'll get a treat."

Fitz had pieces of salmon and a can of green beans cooking when he heard the door open. He hurried over to kiss Katía. "You're looking very pastorly with your blue slacks and white shirt."

"Thanks. I'm going to need to look 'pastorly,'" she said, making air quotes. "What are we going to do if Johnston's ordinance passes?"

"It's too crazy to pass. Plus, when the other council members see how many of their constituents are against it, they'll vote no," Fitz replied.

Katía took a deep breath. "You're right. We've done everything we could. You spread the word to the camps and shelters. I've got the churches on board. Now all we have to do is execute the plan … and hope most of the city shows up."

Fitz hurried to the oven to check the salmon. "And eat."

"I might be too nervous to eat."

"You need energy for tonight's fight," Fitz countered. "Of course, the cats would love your fish."

After supper, Katía drove the church van to the two encampments. It was filled to capacity when they headed toward the meeting. As they neared the parking deck, Katía fell into a long line of vehicles.

"I hope we're not late," Fitz said.

"I hope all these people are here to oppose the ordinance." She reached for Fitz's hand. "It looks like we succeeded!" She let her passengers out in front of the government buildings, then continued on to park in the deck.

"Are you still nervous?" Fitz asked as they walked into the building where the council meeting was being held.

"Not as much as before."

"I trust all these people are against the ordinance instead of for it," Fitz added.

"Now I'm even more nervous!"

Katía stopped and added her name to the list of people requesting to speak at the meeting. She handed the pen to Fitz, and he put it back in its holder.

"Aren't you going to speak?" Katía asked.

"I'm afraid my speaking would hurt the cause more than help it."

Katía rolled her eyes. "Fitz, you know better than that. You're important, and I don't ever want to hear you belittle yourself again."

"Yes, ma'am, but with my history on the force, it might be true. Besides, there are tons of other people signed up."

"Come on." Katía pushed into the packed room and found a place for herself and Fitz to stand along the wall near Sarge and Captain. Katía waved to Luna, Carlos, Zee, and Ben, who were seated in the next-to-last row.

"Thanks for leaving Betsy at home," Fitz nudged Sarge.

"Don't underestimate my bare hands. They're ready if needed."

"Oh, boy. The last thing we need is for you to give them cause to consider this ordinance," Fitz cautioned.

"I'll try to restrain myself," Sarge replied.

Mayor Vernon Thompson rubbed his hand over the bald spot on his head as he gaveled the meeting to order. Brown-haired, at least what was left of it, and brown-eyed, he stood at the lectern in the center of the long table up front and welcomed everyone to the meeting. He looked uncomfortable, his belly pushing against the buttons of his shirt, as he said, "I'm glad you all came out for tonight's council meeting. I understand we have a long list of people wanting to speak tonight, so I'm going to need you to be cooperative, respectful, and quiet so we can give everyone the opportunity they deserve.

Karen Thompson, a forty-four-year-old blond bundle of energy and a council member, worked her way through the crowd and presented the list of people who had signed up to speak.

"Did you sign up to speak?" Fitz whispered to Sarge.

"You know it," she replied loudly enough to draw a scowl from the mayor.

The mayor plodded through two zoning requests, both of which were approved, before calling on Councilman Johnston to present his proposal. Before he reached the lectern, Sarge let out a long, "Boo!"

Mayor Thompson stood back up and spoke, "Ma'am, in our meetings we believe everyone has the right to be heard and the right to be respected. I'll remind you and everyone here that we expect to conduct our business with decorum." He sat back down, and Johnston stepped to the lectern.

After clearing his throat, Johnston began, "I sense that some of you think I'm a villain, but after I present my case, I believe you will see the wisdom of my proposal."

Fitz elbowed Sarge gently and shook his head.

Johnston continued. "As many of you have probably heard, I suffered a break-in at my restaurant the night before last. Fortunately, the money was recovered since the burglar knocked himself out in the restaurant's refrigerator. The man was homeless, or I believe the term we're supposed to use now is unhoused.

"That same night, the very same night, an unhoused person broke into my church and stole money that was being collected for a new shelter that a group of churches plans to build in order to minister to this very population."

Fitz could tell Sarge was getting worked up again and whispered, "Let him have his say."

Johnston was still talking. "While I'm all for helping people, I think it is obvious that these homeless people have become a nuisance and a threat to the hardworking people of our city. They are all breaking the law by being vagrants and loiterers."

Sarge lunged forward, and Fitz grabbed her arm just in time, pulling her back.

Johnston leaned closer to the microphone and said, "The only way I see to solve the problem is to start enforcing the law and put these people in jail. I propose a new ordinance directing law enforcement to arrest any homeless person caught loitering or lingering around businesses or hiding out in encampments. If it becomes necessary, I propose that we petition the National Guard to come in and help with the round-up."

He stood up straight, facing a threatening silence. Fitz saw Sarge was trembling with rage. He noticed the smug expression on Johnston's face wither. Katía was glaring at

Johnston, leaving no question as to how she felt about his words. Fitz took her hand.

Mayor Thompson let the silence simmer a few moments before taking the lectern. "Next we will hear from the people who signed up to speak. Is there anyone who signed up to speak about a topic other than Mr. Johnston's proposal?"

The silence continued.

"OK … Let's begin." He went down the list, calling people to come forward. Finally, he got to Katía, and she went to the lectern.

"Ladies and gentlemen, I'm Katía Bancroft, pastor of St. Luke United Methodist Church, and I am here to speak against Councilman Johnston's proposal. Mr. Johnston suggests that crimes perpetrated by unhoused people are rampant. That couldn't be farther from the truth. In fact, unhoused people commit theft and burglary at a far lower rate than the general population.

"Secondly, he claims that an unhoused person broke into St. Luke's church when in fact no suspect has been identified for that crime. Being on the outskirts of town as our church is makes it even less likely an unhoused person would have been the thief. What happened to innocent till proven guilty?

"Look around you. There are several from the unhoused community here tonight. They are not different from you or me. We are all God's children, and it is our job to support and nurture each other. I'm asking, no, I'm begging you to defeat this proposal. Let's get on with the business of loving each other and taking care of each other."

The room erupted with applause. Mayor Thompson pounded the gavel till people stopped clapping. The rest of the speakers made their cases, then the mayor called for a vote. Johnston's proposal was defeated four to one, with the mayor opting to abstain. The ensuing applause was deafening.

Fitz hugged Katía and felt something wet on his cheek. "Are you crying?"

"Yeah," she said with a smile. "See, you can fight city hall."

Fitz and Katía had to pass Johnston on their way out of the room.

He stated, "Pastor, I can't believe you didn't support me on this, especially after what happened at the church."

"Winslow, I had to do what's right and throwing unhoused people into jail is just wrong. I'm sure you remember Matthew 25:40, 'Truly I tell you, just as you did it to one of the least of these who are members of my family, you did it to me.' Those were Jesus's words."

Johnston glared at her. "Are you saying I need to find another church?" He stomped away.

Katía sighed as Fitz whispered, "That might be good riddance."

Katía burst out laughing. Putting a hand over her mouth, she said, "We need to get these folks home, then get to work figuring out who broke into the church."

"And the wedding," Fitz added.

CHAPTER 7

Katía stopped the van at the trail leading to Sarge's encampment. Sarge stopped at the door. "If he keeps tryin' this stuff, don't be surprised if that councilman's head and Betsy have a talk."

"That will only hurt you, Sarge," Katía replied. "We beat him this time; we can beat him again. I appreciate you for being there."

"You're welcome," Sarge said, stepping off the bus and walking into the darkness with the others from the encampment.

As Katía steered the van toward the church, she said to Fitz, "I hope she doesn't really go after Winslow."

"I don't think she will, at least not now. If he comes to the encampment and tries to throw her out, I'm sure she wouldn't hesitate to take Betsy to his head."

After parking the van and driving back to Katía's house, they found Buffett lounging on one side of the couch with Cotton on the other.

"I see you're making yourself at home," Fitz said to Buffett.

"Meow."

"That's what you have to work on, too," Katía said as she embraced him. "This is your home, too."

After a delicious kiss, Fitz replied, "After living in my car for so long, it's hard to wrap my head around living here. As long as you're here, I'm sure I'll adjust, though."

"Just take a lesson from Buffett. He's a wise cat."

"Yeah, sometimes I think he's smarter than I am."

Katía yawned. "Sorry, it's been a long day. I've never had a church robbed before."

"Yeah, that's awful. I think you need a mug of hot chocolate. I have some in the car."

"That does sound good. There's some in the cabinet. It's closer."

"If you'll come, have a seat, and direct, I'll fix it," Fitz said, tugging her toward the kitchen.

Katía pulled out the list of parishioners they had gathered that morning. "I guess my best bet is to go talk to these folks and pointblank ask them if their relative could have committed the robbery."

"You could end up with some angry parishioners," Fitz said as he poured hot water into the mugs.

"True," she sighed. "How else can I get to the bottom of this, though?"

"As Luna would say, you could leave it up to the police and focus on being a bride preparing for her wedding."

Katía walked up behind Fitz and wrapped her arms around him, nestling into his neck. "I'm prepared, and I can't wait! I can't think of anything else that needs tending to wedding-wise. How about you?"

Fitz tugged his beard and patted her arms. "You're right. I think everything is covered."

"There is one surprise that hasn't arrived yet."

"What's that?"

Hugging him tighter, Katía said, "If I told you, it wouldn't be a surprise, would it?"

They sat down at the table with the hot chocolate. Fitz slipped a few M&Ms into his mouth while she wasn't looking.

After a sip, Katía asked, "Seriously, do you really think I shouldn't go around asking questions?"

"I'd say doing so is a good way to get yourself run off from the church," Fitz replied. "Plus, the deputies will be going around asking the same questions."

Katía scrunched her eyebrows. "I hadn't thought of that, … but people might be more willing to open up to me."

Fitz tugged his beard. "It sounds like your mind is made up. Want me to come along?"

"I thought you'd never ask."

The next morning, Katía started calling the parishioners on her list promptly at 10:30. She arranged times to visit with each one who answered. At 11:00, Fitz arrived, and they headed to the first house.

Katía took a deep breath. "This is Earl and Faye Higginbotham. Their grandson got out of a drug rehab program last month. He's living with them. I hope he's at work now," she explained to Fitz before getting out of her Prius.

Katía knocked, and Faye, a seventy-two-year-old whose auburn hair revealed gray roots if examined closely, opened the door. "Hello, Pastor. It's good of you to come by. Hey, Fitz."

Katía gave her points for remembering Fitz's name. When they were seated in the living room, she began. "I'm sure you've heard about the break-in at the church." Faye nodded. "The deputy who came out when I reported it wanted a list of parishioners who might have family members with drug or mental health issues. She was thinking the break-in had to have been committed by someone who knew we were collecting the offering."

"So you told them about Joey," Faye stated flatly.

"I had to, Faye. I wanted to give you a heads-up that they might be asking questions."

"Well, you're too late. Somebody came by yesterday afternoon."

Katía's nerves tensed. *How can I find out what she told them?* "I'm sorry they bothered you, but they're just doing their job." Katía squelched the temptation to ask what Faye had told the deputy.

"I know. Once you've committed a crime, it always follows you. Joey works a nightshift cleaning job at the hospital. After he got off, he came home and went to bed. He was here by seven-thirty that morning, so I don't see how he'd have had time to break into the church."

"That's a relief," Katía replied. "It sounds like Joey has started off on the right foot. How are you and Earl doing?"

"Oh, we're fine. I'm actually enjoying having Joey here. I've gotten to spend more time with him than I have since he was a child. Earl's out in the shop doing some kind of woodworking project. I can get him if you like."

"No, that's fine. Can we have a prayer before we go?"

"Sure."

Katía prayed, "Dear loving God, we're grateful that Joey is getting back on his feet and pray you will be with him during this journey. Bless Earl and Faye with your strength and guidance as well. Amen."

After shutting the car door, Katía said, "Whew. That wasn't so bad."

"Nope. One down, twelve to go," Fitz replied.

The next house they came to, a sprawling brick ranch, belonged to Ted and Tammy Williams.

"I imagine Ted'll be at work. Tammy was a teacher till she had to retire early to help care for her brother. He has PTSD and depression and lives in their basement," Katía explained before they got out of the car.

Tammy led them into the den and offered to fix sandwiches for lunch.

"No, thank you. We'll eat later," Katía replied. "We won't take much of your time." She went through her spiel about wanting to alert people to the fact that a deputy might come by to question them regarding their relative.

"What makes you think Terrance would do such a thing? I can't believe you would suspect him," Tammy fumed, sweeping her long blond hair over her shoulder.

"I don't suspect him. The deputy asked me to give her any names of people who had relatives with psych or drug issues," Katía replied, trying to deflect Tammy's anger onto the sheriff's department.

Tammy sighed. "I'm sorry. I don't mean to be angry with you. I just get tired of people assuming Terrance is bad just because he has… his issue. He's staying on his medicines and has been doing well, at least for him."

Katía decided to press. "I'm glad to hear that. So he was here Monday night then?"

"I'm sure he was. He goes to his support group on Mondays and isn't usually back before Ted and I go to bed. If the deputy wants assurance, I can show them our security camera's footage."

"Deputy James seemed right thorough, so don't be offended if she asks to see it. She'll just be doing her job," Fitz added.

Irritation flickered in Tammy's eyes before she spoke again. "How are the wedding plans coming?"

Katía grinned radiantly. "I think everything is set. We have to pick up Brian at the airport next Thursday. After that, I think we can cruise on through."

"That's great," Tammy said. "I'm happy for you. As long as this deputy doesn't have us pinned down for questioning, we'll be there."

Katía apologized again and said a prayer before she and Fitz left. Back in the car, Fitz said, "In the deputy's eyes, Terrance will remain a suspect unless their footage shows otherwise. So far you've only irritated one out of two."

"Oh, hush and pull us out some granola bars and waters from the lunch bag."

By the end of the afternoon, they had made it to eight of the thirteen parishioners on Katía's list. Two, assuming Terrance proved to be home, were unaccounted for. Katía texted Deputy James what she had learned.

"I'm bushed," Katía said after leaving the last house. "I think you're going to have to treat me to dinner tonight."

"Gladly," Fitz replied. "Something just occurred to me."

"What's that?"

"You went to a meeting today about the shelter. Did any of the other churches know about your offering?"

"They all do. So?"

"So it could be anyone from any of those churches. I think we're barking up the wrong tree."

Katía sighed. "So you're saying we wasted this whole afternoon."

"Not at all. I got to spend it with you."

"Aw. Now what do we do?"

"We could just let it go and let the sheriff's office worry about it. It was just money."

Katía scrunched her eyes together. "I feel like I have an obligation to the church to find out what happened."

"In that case, let's hope an idea comes up over dinner," Fitz said.

CHAPTER 8

atía yawned again and said, "I'm too tired to decide what to eat."

"How about we get takeout at Longstreet and go to your house?" Fitz suggested.

"You're almost a genius. Once you start saying 'our house,' you'll qualify as one. I want to go in and see what they have instead of ordering from the car."

They went through the buffet line and made their selections. Katía stopped after turning from the cashier. Not noticing, Fitz bumped into her. "Sorry," he said.

She had spotted Councilman Johnston and his wife, Stacey, a blond-haired, green-eyed southern belle, sitting at a table. "Should I mention the vote again?"

"I wouldn't. He'll think you're rubbing salt into his wound," Fitz replied.

He followed as Katía approached them. "Good evening," Katía said. "How are y'all tonight?"

"Hey, Pastor," Stacey smiled. "It's always a joy to see you, and you, too, Fitz. We're doin' great and enjoyin' some chicken tenders. How about y'all? All excited about the upcoming weddin', I'm sure."

"That we are," Katía replied. "I can't believe it's a week from Saturday!"

"We're excited to share in your special day," Stacey said. "Let me know if there is anything I can do to help."

"Thanks, I'll keep that in mind."

Fitz wanted to reach for M&Ms but forced himself to refrain. *If the councilman would say something, it would help.*

Stacey said, "Isn't it a shame about the offerin'. I've seen people puttin' in contributions. It would have helped a lot toward gettin' the shelter off the ground. Of course, Winslow's a bit disappointed he didn't get the property, but there are plenty of other places to start a restaurant, aren't there, dear?" She patted his leg.

"I'm sure I can find a suitable location."

"Fitz and I need to get to the house before this cools off. You two have a blessed evening."

"You, too," Stacey and Winslow said together.

Once they were back inside Katía's Prius, Fitz said, "That was tense."

"I noticed you hit the M&Ms on the way to the car," Katía chuckled.

Back at the house, Buffett greeted them with a meow and leg rubs.

"Of course we brought you something," Fitz said.

Cotton and Snow joined in the greeting, which quickly turned to begging.

"Buffett's teaching them to beg," Katía said.

"At least they have a master teacher," Fitz laughed. He broke up the hamburger patty he had bought for the cats.

As he leaned to put it on the floor, Katía said, "Wait! What are you doing?"

"I'm giving the cats their prize," he said, stopping in mid-bend.

"Um, I always put it on a saucer before putting it down."

"Oh." Fitz straightened up. "Hang on a minute, you three. Where are the saucers?"

Katía pointed to the cabinet where she kept them.

"I'd just put this on the seat for Buffett. He licks it clean. You're losing a lot of free mopping by using these," Fitz chuckled as he pulled out the saucers and put a third of the hamburger patty on each one. Setting the saucers down, he said to Buffett, "It looks like we're going to have to learn to be a bit more refined."

To the sound of purring, he sat down to eat with Katía. While taking his first bite, Fitz heard his phone pinging with an incoming text.

"That's odd," he said as he fished the phone from his pocket. "It's Sarge. She says there's word on the street that Harley was knocked on the head, then dragged into a car the night of the restaurant robbery."

"That's awful. I wonder if someone forced him to commit the robbery."

"I don't know, but I'm going to talk to Sarge."

Having finished supper, kissed Katía goodnight, and loaded Buffett into the car, Fitz parked on the side of the road near Sarge's encampment.

He explained to Buffett, "I'm leaving you to guard the car. I'll be back in a little while."

He found Sarge and three men sitting beside a fire.

"Pull up a log and take a load off," Sarge said.

"Hey, Sarge," Fitz said as he sat down next to her. "Tell me about this rumor you heard about Harley."

"You don't waste words on small talk, do ya?" Sarge replied. "Somebody, and they didn't say who it was, claims they saw it happen."

"Did they say where?"

"Said he was walking down Industrial. Probably had been to the store and was comin' back to camp."

"Is that all we know as of now?"

"Yep, that's all I got." Sarge poked at the logs with a stick, sending sparks flying.

"I appreciate your help. I think I'm going to try to get in to talk to Harley tomorrow." Fitz stood to leave.

"You should stick around. We'll break out the s'mores and sing Kumbaya soon."

"I'd love to see that," Fitz laughed. He walked back to his Highlander and greeted Buffett. It was 9:45 p.m.

"I say let's sleep at Walmart tonight. That OK with you?"

"Meow."

"We only have a few nights left to sleep in the car … I guess we could always sleep in Katía's driveway if we miss the car too much."

Buffett kept quiet.

"So you think you'll stay in the house, huh?"

"Meow."

"I see. In the morning, I have to see if I can get Ben to hack into the traffic cameras again." He texted Katía about what he had learned from Sarge, then drove to Walmart.

Fitz arrived at Laurel Park the next morning well before the sun got out of bed. He went through his routine of washing up, tending to Buffett's litter, and putting down some treats. "I think you woke me up too early."

"Meow."

"Well, why'd you do that?"

Buffett didn't respond, being busy eating the treats. When he was finished, Fitz led him over to the closest picnic table. Pulling up the WDUN stream on his phone, he heard, "Join us at nine o'clock for an interview with Winslow Johnston. Now, back to the news."

Fitz cut off the stream when Zee pulled up, groaning as he stood from the car. "Am I late, or are you early?"

"I'm early. Someone was eager to get the day started." He pointed to Buffett.

"They do have minds of their own."

"I'll watch King while you clean up," Fitz offered.

"Thanks."

Ben pulled in while Zee was washing up. "Good morning," he said as he got out to leash up Snickers.

"Morning," Fitz said.

Ben and Snickers joined him at the picnic table.

"I've got an issue I want to see if you'll help resolve," Fitz said.

"That sounds cryptic. What is it?"

"There's word that the man who was arrested for breaking into Johnston's restaurant was hit over the head and dragged into a car the night the break-in happened."

"That is an issue. How can I help?"

"Could we check to see if it got caught on one of the traffic cameras?"

Ben smiled. "I'd love to."

CHAPTER 9

The park pals finished walking the trail that gorgeous Thursday morning, and Katía asked Fitz if he wanted to go visiting more of the parishioners on her list.

"I'd love to, but Ben and I have a date," Fitz replied.

"Oh?" Katía said, eyebrows raising.

Fitz pulled his beard while trying to decide whether to tell Katía what they had planned.

"Are you trying to keep secrets from me already?"

"You should know that we women have ways of finding out what men are hiding. You might as well surrender," Luna laughed.

"OK," Fitz said. "Ben's going to see if we can find footage of Harley's abduction on the traffic cameras."

Katía's hands went to her hips. "And why would you not want to tell me that?"

"Oooh, you done stirred up a hornets' nest," Zee chuckled.

"I didn't want to worry you," Fitz said, then popped M&Ms into his mouth.

"Why would that worry me?" Katía asked.

"Because it suggests someone forced Harley to rob that restaurant. If that's the case, we have a much bigger problem than it appears on the surface."

"What do you mean?"

"I mean we could have an organized crime ring who have decided to force unhoused folks to do robberies," Fitz explained.

"Oh, me," Zee said.

"Wait, what?" Luna asked.

"Sarge got word that someone knocked out Harley and dragged him into a car the night of the restaurant break-in." Fitz explained.

"That sounds serious," Luna replied.

Katía embraced Fitz. "You be careful and don't let anybody snatch you. … You either, Zee."

"Me and King'll keep our eyes peeled," Zee replied.

Katía let go of Fitz and said, "I need to get to the office. Let me know what you find out."

"I'll make sure he does," Ben said. "You want to come to the house with us, Zee?"

"I'd love to."

As Katía was getting into her car, Fitz said, "Oh, yeah. Johnston is giving an interview on WDUN at nine."

"Thanks. I'll tune in and see what he has to say."

Ben put on a pot of coffee while Zee let King and Snickers out in the backyard. Fitz unleashed Buffett.

"You got any pre-wedding jitters yet?" Ben asked.

"You're givin' up a lot for her," Zee quipped. "Your mansion, the freedom to sleep anywhere you like, the miserable summer heat."

"I think I'll adjust," Fitz said.

Ben settled down at the computer. "Help yourself to some bagels and cream cheese. It'll take a while to get into the system."

"I know … 'Don't hover over my shoulder, either,'" Fitz added. He found the cream cheese while Zee located the bagels. "Want us to fix you one?"

"I thought you'd never ask," Ben replied. "I sure hope they never update their security on this site. We seem to need it a lot."

Fitz placed a bagel and a mug of coffee on the counter for Ben, then checked his watch.

"You got somewhere to be?" Ben asked.

"No, I just want to hear what Johnston has to say this morning."

"Need a radio?"

"No, thanks. I can stream it on the phone."

Ben went back to working on the computer.

Zee swallowed a bite of bagel. "Seriously, what's it like to think about livin' in a house after all these years?"

Fitz took a bite to give himself a minute. *I'd rather not talk about it, but I'm supposed to be getting past that.* "It's exciting and guilt-ridden. On one hand, I feel like I'm betraying you and the rest of the unhoused community. Why should I get to live in a comfortable home? On the other hand, there's Katía. I get to be with her. I won't lie, sleeping in a bed sounds wonderful. Other than when I've slept here, I haven't been able to really stretch out in a long time."

Setting down his coffee mug, Zee replied, "Stretching out does sound nice. Don't feel guilty on my account. I'm happy for you. Plus, you can invite me for supper every now and then."

"We'll definitely do that."

"I'm in," Ben said. "I hope you have an idea where this guy was abducted."

"Sarge said it was on Industrial Boulevard. I'd start at Queen City Parkway and work south. He frequents a convenience store, there." Fitz answered.

"Sounds like a plan." Ben located the camera footage for that intersection. "Any idea what time?"

"All I know is that it was nighttime. Harley would have been on foot, so look for a pedestrian rather than vehicles."

"That makes it easier, but it's still a lot of time to cover. I'm going to start at eight o'clock."

Fitz got up to look over Ben's shoulder. He checked his watch and saw he still had ten minutes until Johnston's interview. Scanning the footage as it sped by, Fitz noted several people on foot entering the convenience store on the corner. There was also a package store across the street.

Fitz saw a tall, thin man who looked like Harley. "Pause it."

Ben zoomed in on the guy Fitz pointed to.

"That's him. Let it roll, and let's see what we get."

Zee looked over the other shoulder. "That's Harley all right."

They watched as he crossed the street and continued till he was out of the camera's sight.

"No abduction. How about the next camera?" Fitz asked.

Ben worked the computer. "It looks like the next camera is at Aviation Boulevard. That's past the encampment, isn't it?"

"Yeah. We didn't learn a thing," Fitz said.

"We learned one thing," Ben added. "Whoever did it was smart enough to avoid getting caught on camera."

"True." Fitz checked his watch again. "Let's see what that councilman is ranting about this morning."

He opened the stream of the broadcast just in time to hear the announcer introducing his guest.

"We are happy to have Winslow Johnston with us this morning. He represents District One on the city council. Councilman, we're glad you could join us this morning."

"Thank you, Russ. It's always good to talk with you."

"What can you tell us about the break-in at your restaurant?"

"Russ, I think you know as much as I do at this point. When I went into The Oasis on Monday morning, I discovered the restaurant had been broken into. I found a man lying unconscious in the refrigerator. He had the money from the register with him," Johnston explained.

"Why do you think he was in the refrigerator?"

"It turns out this was a homeless man. I assume he either heard me unlocking the door and tried to hide or was looking for food. Either way, he seems to have tripped and hit his head.

"Russ, let me point out that this incident just further underscores the epidemic of crime caused by the homeless population in our town. People are being robbed right and left. A homeless person even broke into my church and stole nearly thirty-six hundred dollars that was earmarked for a new shelter in Gainesville. Instead of building a new shelter, I think we need to expand the jail and house this group of criminals there."

Fitz cut off the broadcast. "I've heard enough of this guy. How could he possibly jump to the conclusion that an unhoused person broke into the church? Nobody knows who did it yet." He dug some M&Ms from his pocket.

"I don't like his attitude," Zee said. "Just because someone broke into his restaurant doesn't mean there's an epidemic. In fact, I ain't heard of any other crimes committed by our crew."

"I'm not going to let him get away with this," Fitz said. "I'm going to prove him wrong."

"How are you going to do that?" Ben asked.

"To start with, I'm going to see Harley and find out what really happened."

CHAPTER 10

Fitz parked at the city jail at 1:45 p.m., fifteen minutes ahead of his scheduled visit with Harley. He removed his pocketknife in order to get through security. Next, he decided to put some M&Ms into a zip-lock bag to make it easier when he emptied his pockets. *On second thought, I'd better leave the M&Ms here. They might think they're laced with drugs.* He ate a few before setting the bag on the console. "Stay out of those, Buffett."

After going through security, he signed in and sat down to wait. *If someone used Harley as a decoy, why did they leave the money with him? Could they have stolen something other than money?*

A door opened, and a woman called, "Mr. Fitzgerald." Fitz stood, realizing he was the only one in the waiting area. He followed her back to find Harley waiting in a booth. He picked up the phone.

"Hey, Harley, how are you doing?"

"I've been better."

"They treating you all right?"

"Yeah, so far."

Fitz tugged his beard. "How did you end up in that restaurant?"

"I don't know, man. I remember walking down the street with my new bottle of Mogen David. I get one every week. Two guys came up and asked me where I lived. I told 'em I got no address. Next thing I know, I wake up in that cold fridge. The cops came and arrested me. Said I was robbin' the place."

Fitz asked, "So you don't remember anyone forcing you to go into the restaurant?"

"No, man. I don't remember nothin' till I woke up cold."

Fitz worked his mind. *There has to be something I can ask that will trigger his memory.* "How did you get into the restaurant?"

"Fitz, you ain't listenin'. I don't know nothin' from the time I was on the street talkin' to those two guys till I woke up in the fridge."

"Did your head hurt?"

"Yeah, man. It was killin' me, and I got a knot right here," he said, rubbing the back of his head.

"Do you have any idea why someone would want to frame you for the break-in? Have you made anybody mad lately?"

"Fitz, you know me. I mostly keep to myself. I sit around the fire with Sarge and some of the others, but we ain't had no fights. As far as I know, they're the only ones knows I exist."

"Do you remember what the two guys on the street looked like?"

"Not really. They was White. I was tryin' to keep my head down so they'd leave me alone. Didn't get much of a look at 'em. Why you askin' all these questions?"

"I want to try to help you," Fitz said. "I don't believe you broke into that restaurant."

"I don't believe I did either. If you could get me outta here, I'd be grateful."

"Have they assigned you an attorney yet?"

"Yeah. I'm supposed to see her today at three."

"Do you remember the name?"

"It's Lauren Hamilton. I hope she's worth her salt."

"Me, too. They're going to run me out of here in a couple of minutes. Is there anything I can do for you?" Fitz asked.

"Let Sarge know what happened. They give me three squares a day and a bed, so I'm OK, for now. But I sure don't wanna stay here."

"Keep the faith. I'll do what I can to find out who's behind this."

"Thanks, man."

Fitz left the jail, sat in his car, and ate M&Ms while pondering what to do next. He pulled out a small notepad and jotted notes:

1. Find out who the arresting officer was.
2. Did they find evidence of him hitting his head in the cooler?
3. Was anything else stolen that they are keeping quiet about? Stole more money than owned up to? Stole

something else councilman doesn't want public to know about? Prize steaks?

4. Who would need to deflect suspicion about the break-in?

While he was writing, he heard a car door slam. Looking up, he saw a smartly-dressed, gaunt, black-haired woman walking toward the jail. *I bet that's her.*

He jumped out of the car and called, "Ma'am."

She turned and, though Fitz couldn't hear it, he saw her sigh.

"Lauren Hamilton?"

She nodded.

"I'm a friend of your client, Harley." Fitz approached her. "I believe his story and believe that he is innocent. I'll be happy to help in any way I can. I'm a retired police officer."

Blue eyes narrowed with suspicion, she said, "I don't usually need help, but I appreciate the offer." She turned and marched into the jail.

Fitz's shoulders sagged. *Was it the beard?* He walked back to the car and looked over the notes he had made. *If Harley's telling the truth, then who would plant him in a restaurant refrigerator and why? As unpleasant as it sounds, I need to talk to Johnston.*

Fitz startled at a knock on his windshield. He looked up to see the chief of police, Amos Arnold, waving. Cranking the car, he rolled down the window. "Hey, Chief."

"Hey, Fitz, you been behaving yourself lately?"

"As best I can. How about you? How are you doing?"

Arnold removed his brown fedora, which matched his brown hair, and resettled it onto his head. "I'm good. Just the usual problems of policing this town. I hear congratulations are in order. I'm happy for you on your upcoming wedding."

"Thanks! It's going to be quite an adjustment."

"I'm sure Pastor Bancroft can whip you into shape," the chief chuckled. "I have to get inside. Take care of yourself."

"You, too," Fitz said as Arnold turned and strode toward the jail.

Checking his watch, Fitz saw it was nearly three o'clock. He started to call Katía, then decided a text would be better just in case she was still talking with a parishioner. "How's it going? I'll see you at supper."

When she didn't text back, he decided she was tied up. "Buffett, what should we do till supper time? … I've got an idea. Let's go by the grocery store and get stuff to make some chicken Alfredo."

"Meow."

"You're always up for chicken."

After stopping by the store, Fitz pulled into Katía's driveway. "I can't believe we're going to live here in a little over a week." He sat with his heart doing somersaults. Buffett rubbed his chin. "Thanks. I'm glad you'll help me through this transition. We can always come out and sleep in the car if we miss it too much."

"Meow."

He punched in the code to the electric lock and walked in to find Cotton and Snow waiting. They greeted Buffett and rubbed against Fitz's legs.

"Y'all are quick learners. Come on." He set the groceries on the counter and placed three small piles of treats on the floor. Fitz smiled as he listened to the purring that accompanied the cats' eating.

Checking his phone, he saw Katía still had not texted back, prompting worry to settle in. He started opening cabinets till he found the pots he would need for boiling the noodles and warming the sauce. *It's too early to start cooking.*

Fitz sat down on one of the two kitchen chairs, then immediately stood back up. He wandered down the hall and looked into the bedroom. Standing in the doorway, he wondered if she let the cats sleep with her. *I hope so. I'd miss sleeping with Buffett.*

He remembered his old house and wondered how much money was in the mutual fund account into which he had placed the money from its sale. He didn't check. Instead, he ambled to the den. *Maybe I should sit in here.* Buffett was waiting for him on the couch. Cotton was on the other end, and Snow was curled up in the recliner. Fitz sat down, leaned his head back, and petted Buffett.

The sound of the door's opening awoke Fitz. He looked around, confused. *Where am I?*

"Hey, Fitz!" Katía's voice sounded, bringing clarity to his confusion.

He stood up. "I'm in the den."

"You look like I woke you up from a nap. Sorry about that," she said, coming in for a hug.

"I'll admit it; I fell asleep. How was your day?"

"Better now." Katía jammed her purse onto the end table.

"You seem mad."

"I am. I talked with some irritating parishioners today."

"What's wrong?"

"I don't want to talk about it," she answered.

"Hey, that's supposed to be my line."

Katía's scrunched eyebrows softened into a smile. "True, and I don't like it when you say that. I guess the shoe's on the other foot."

"Well, what's wrong?"

Katía took a deep breath. "Three of the parishioners I talked to today hinted they thought it is wrong for me to marry an unhoused person. I wanted to slap them, but I refrained."

Fitz took her hand. "I'm sorry they upset you."

"It's just not right. It's not Christian, either."

"So who's wrong in this situation?"

"They are," Katía replied.

"Then it's their problem. I'm sure there are more of them out there. You just have to let it roll on off."

"Like water off a duck, I know. But as their pastor, I'm supposed to fix them."

"I don't think so," Fitz said. "I think you're just supposed to point them in the right direction."

Katía hugged him again. "Did anyone ever tell you you're a wise soul?"

"I don't think so." Fitz enjoyed the embrace before saying, "I bought stuff to make chicken Alfredo for supper. You relax, and I'll go get started."

"A girl could get used to this kind of treatment."

"I hope so," Fitz said.

While eating, they shared what they had found out during the day.

"I didn't find any more potential suspects," Katía said. "Only folks who need an attitude adjustment."

"Harley said he has no idea how he ended up in the restaurant's refrigerator, but the knot on his head suggests he was knocked out."

"Do you think he's telling the truth?"

"I do. He seemed totally perplexed about what happened."

"It looks like we're facing two battles. We have to find out who broke into the church before Winslow convinces the city to round up the unhoused folks, and we have to find out what really happened with Harley before he ends up in jail."

"That sums it up. The only question is how do we do all that?"

CHAPTER 11

As usual, Fitz was the first of the park pals to arrive at Laurel Park. The lack of stars promised a gray Friday morning. After cleaning up in the bathroom, he scooped Buffett's litter.

"After the wedding, I'll still take you with me when I go places," he explained to Buffett. "You won't be stuck in the house all the time."

"Meow."

"We'll still come walk around the park."

"Meow."

Fitz and Katía had decided to go to St. Simons Island for their honeymoon. It was close enough that they could make the drive after the wedding.

The rest of the park pals trickled in, Luna being the last to arrive. She hurried over to the others, who were waiting by a picnic table. "I can't believe the rehearsal dinner is a week from today! Are you ready to fire up the grill?"

Ben smiled. "It's a little early to light it up just yet, but it'll be smoking next Friday."

Luna punched Ben on the shoulder. "You know what I mean. We'll head to my house right after we finish running through the ceremony. The rehearsal's at five-thirty, right?"

Katía laughed. "Luna, I believe you're more excited about the wedding than I am. Yeah, it's at five-thirty down by the lake. It shouldn't take more than fifteen minutes, thirty at the most."

"I think we're all excited about this weddin'," Zee added. "Finally, something good's happenin' around here instead of people's lives bein' in jeopardy. I was beginnin' to think this park was cursed."

"We have had our share of adventure over the last year. Any word on the break-in at your church?" Ben asked.

"Not other than Winslow trying to frame a residentially-challenged person for it. He made another public statement to that effect yesterday." Katía sighed. "Now you've got me saying residentially-challenged."

Fitz laughed. "It is a good term, you have to admit."

"I wonder why Winslow's so sure it's an unhoused person?" Luna asked.

"Yeah, he sure seems to have it in for us folks. You'd think he'd be like the other politicians and blame everything on immigrants," Zee said.

"He does seem to be against the unhoused community," Ben added. "Fitz and I heard his broadcast yesterday."

"It's just Winslow. I think his restaurant is on a path the unhoused frequently walk, and he's afraid they'll scare away customers," Katía explained.

Zee put his arm around Fitz's shoulder. "We are a scary bunch." The others laughed.

"Seriously, guys, I want to find out who broke into the church before Winslow gets an innocent person put in jail," Katía said.

"Honey, you have a wedding to worry about. Let the sheriff's office figure this out," Luna coaxed.

"I know," Katía sighed. "But the wedding is ready. All I have to do now is wait." She took Fitz's hand.

Snickers tugged on her leash. "Snickers says it's time to get walking," Ben said.

As they walked, they talked about the wedding. Katía would be picking up her dress Monday. Luna went over the rehearsal dinner menu. Ben would be grilling pork tenderloin. All the time, Fitz's mind kept wondering about Harley.

"Fitz, you sure are quiet this morning," Luna observed. When he didn't respond, she punched him in the shoulder.

"What?" he replied.

"What has you so distracted?" Luna asked.

"Harley."

"What about Harley?" Luna asked.

"I think he's being framed."

"Why would anyone want to frame him for a robbery when nothing was actually stolen?" Ben said.

"Nothing that we know about, anyway," Fitz added.

"What do you mean?" Katía asked.

"Sometimes victims will keep the report of what was really taken hidden if they don't want it to get out," Fitz explained.

"You mean the robber might not have been after money?" Ben asked.

"I'd've been after steaks," Zee chuckled, rubbing his hands together.

Fitz added, "I'm convinced Harley didn't break into the restaurant. He said he was walking down the street when two guys came up to him. The next thing he remembered was waking up in the refrigerator with a knot on his head. I think something bigger is going on here."

King barked and Snickers pulled Ben forward when a squirrel lingered near the trail. "You could warn me before you do that," Ben scolded.

Buffett kept his tail high and pranced like he was way above the dogs.

"If you don't think they were after money, then what?" Ben asked.

"That's the question, isn't it? That and who did it," Fitz replied. "This reeks of organized crime."

"In Gainesville? That's hard to believe," Luna replied.

"Why would someone in organized crime target Winslow?" Katía asked. "He's just a city councilman."

"With the lake and big businesses moving in, there's a lot of opportunity for shady deals," Ben observed. "The question is, how can we figure out who did it?"

"I think my first step is to talk to the arresting officer and see if I can find out exactly what they found at the scene," Fitz said.

"Poor Geraldine. She's gonna get another call," Zee teased.

"Actually, I'll have to go through Gainesville City Police this time," Fitz replied. "I think I'll need some help. They're not real fond of me."

"I'll go in and ask," Ben offered.

"On second thought, I think I'll pay a visit to Serena."

"The reporter at the Times?" Ben asked.

"That's the one. She's always interested in tips for a good story."

"How about Katía's church? What can we do about that?" Luna asked, tightening her ponytail.

"I hate to say it, but with no security footage and no witnesses, we may never find out who broke into the church," Fitz replied.

"That's just great," Katía huffed. "I want that money back. The shelter's going to need it."

"There has to be something we can do," Luna said.

They arrived back at the cars, and Katía gave Fitz a kiss. "I need to get to the office."

"I thought Friday was your day off," Luna said.

"It usually is, but I'm behind on my sermon after all the business with the break-in. I'll just work a couple of hours."

"I have to get going, too," Luna said, and the two women departed.

While watching them drive off, Zee said, "Mind if I come along with you to see that reporter? I'd love to meet the woman who helped save my life last winter."

"Sure, come on," Fitz replied.

"I think I'll join you, too. I have an empty day ahead of me," Ben added. "I'm happy to drive."

They loaded Snickers and King into the back of Ben's Outback. Zee opened the door to get into the back, but Fitz protested.

"Your long legs need the front. Buffett and I'll fit back here just fine."

When they arrived at the front desk of the Times, Fitz asked for Serena Granger, and they sat down to wait.

"Hey, Fitz! Ben! Sorry I kept you waiting. I was on the phone," Serena said as she strode across the lobby, her sandy blond hair pulled back into a ponytail.

She shook Fitz and Ben's hands, then extended her hand to Zee. "Hi. Serena Granger."

"I'm Zee. I'm one of the ones you helped save last winter when that deranged doctor was on the loose. I sure am grateful."

"Well, it's certainly nice to meet you. I'm glad I could do a little bit to help out. I ended up getting an award for that story," Serena said with a smile. "Come on back and tell me what's up." She led the way back to her desk and pulled up two more chairs.

"We may have another doozy of a story for you," Fitz began. He explained Harley's situation. "I believe Harley, which means someone abducted him and stuck him in that refrigerator to cover up what was really going on."

"I see," Serena said, looking up from the notes she had written. "Not that I don't trust your hunches, but there isn't anything I can report here."

"Not yet, anyway," Fitz replied. "But there could be if you help me out a little."

Serena's eyes narrowed. "What do you have in mind?"

"I need to find out who the arresting officer was in Harley's case. If you would call up and say you want to do a story on the case and find out who it was, it would help," Fitz grinned.

"And how is that going to give me a story?"

Fitz replied, "If it turns out that there is an organized crime ring working out of Gainesville, you will have already started your research."

Serena tapped her pen on the desk. "It can't hurt to make a few calls. I'll update you on anything I discover if you'll return the favor."

"We'd be happy to do that," Fitz said.

Serena shook their hands. "I'll be in touch."

CHAPTER 12

Armed with the name of the officer who had arrested Harley and the knowledge that she was on the day shift, Fitz hurried to the police station to catch her before shift change. He parked and rushed toward the door. Just as he was reaching for the handle, it opened. The officer who walked out the door had Abramson on her name tag.

Fitz pivoted, ended up walking beside her, and said, "Officer Abramson?"

"That's me, but I'm headed out."

"I'm Fitz Fitzgerald," he said, hurrying to keep up with her. "You were the arresting officer for the guy found unconscious in the refrigerator at The Oasis."

"You're right about that, too." She kept walking.

"Would you mind if I ask you a couple of questions about the crime scene?"

She stopped and looked Fitz over. Short and stocky with frizzy black hair, she had a demeanor that made most people back away. Fitz stood and waited.

Finally she said, "Don't tell me … he's a friend of yours, and you think he's innocent."

"You're exactly right," Fitz said, knowing he had just a few seconds to give her a reason to talk with him. He hoped that playing to officers' common fear of arresting the wrong person would be the trick. "I believe he was abducted and planted in the refrigerator as a decoy."

She scowled at him, then said, "I'm listening."

"Did you find any broken shelves or anything that suggested he had hit his head in the refrigerator?"

"No. I assume he tripped and hit his head on the floor."

"Where was the head injury?" Fitz asked.

"On the back of his head."

"If he had tripped, wouldn't he have hit the front of his head?" Fitz suggested.

"Unless he fell backwards."

"How much blood was on the floor?"

Officer Abramson paused. "If I remember correctly, there was only a small smear, but I'd have to check the crime scene photos to be sure."

"From the bandage I saw on Harley's head, there should have been a lot of blood." Fitz stopped to let her make the connection.

"Unless he was knocked unconscious somewhere else," she said. She pulled out a pad and wrote some notes. "I'm back on duty in the morning, so I'll check this out. Right now I have to go."

Having already written his name and number on a slip of paper, Fitz handed it to her. "I'd be grateful if you would let me know what you find." She took the paper and headed to her car.

Fitz watched her leave, the gears turning in his mind. *At least I got the seed planted. She won't call me.* Eyeing the building, he remembered when he had gone in and out those doors wearing a uniform. Briefly, he missed the hustle of those days but thought better of it when he remembered the stress.

Now what to do? He headed to the car to find Buffett asleep on the dash. As he opened the door, his phone rang.

"Hey, Sweetie," Katía said. "I vote for going out to eat tonight. How about you?"

"That sounds good to me. Any suggestions as to where?"

"I'm craving Mexican. How about El Sombrero?"

"Perfect. Buffett and I are going to stop by the library. I'll see you at your house."

"Great. Wait, it's our house. See you soon!"

Fitz walked into the library and headed upstairs to read the paper. While he could pull it up on his phone, he much preferred having the actual paper in his hand. He scanned the front page. The headlines included: "Inland Port Continues to Take Shape," and "Another Large Subdivision Slated for South Hall."

He scanned through these quickly and turned the page. An article on page three caught his attention: "Rash of

Robberies by the Unhoused Continues." Fitz sat up and leaned toward the paper to read.

"In what is the third break-in this week alleged to have been committed by a member of the unhoused community, Heinrich and Josie Friedrich returned to their home after attending a movie to find Nate Powell unconscious in their bedroom closet. Police surmise that Powell was attempting to open the safe when he fell and knocked himself out. Deputy Baker stated that they are still awaiting blood test results to determine if drugs or alcohol played a role in Wilkins being unconscious.

"The Friedrichs, owners of a restaurant in Flowery Branch, stated that they are thankful nothing was stolen, but that they still feel violated."

Fitz tugged his beard and pulled out M&Ms. "This is ridiculous," he muttered before remembering he was in the library. *There's no way! What are they not telling us? I need the rest of the story.*

He checked to see which journalist had written the article. It was Serena Granger. Putting the paper back, he hurried out of the library and dialed the newspaper office.

"Serena Granger, please." The receptionist transferred his call, and it went to her voicemail. "Hey, Serena, it's Fitz. I have a couple of questions about your article on the break-in at the Friedrichs' home. When you get a chance, please give me a call."

He left his number and disconnected. *I won't hear anything from her till at least Monday.* Popping a few more M&Ms into his mouth, he headed to Katía's house and found her already there. He knocked on the door and tried to quell the anger that had been brewing since he left the library.

Opening the door, Katía said, "Fitz, when are you going to stop doing that?"

"Doing what?"

"You don't have to knock, you know. Just come on in."

"Oh." He walked into the house and into Katía's embrace. "I missed you today."

"I missed you, too," she replied.

She pulled her head back and looked into his eyes. "What's wrong?"

Fitz said, "I don't want to talk about it." The look on Katía's face checked him, so he told her about the article in the paper. Next he said, "Something bad is going on. I don't believe any of these break-ins were committed by residentially-challenged people. The one today is just like Harley's incident."

"I texted Diann today. She said the same thing you did … that we're not likely to catch whoever robbed the church since there is no evidence to get leads from. I wish we had installed the security system last year when the council talked about it. They decided it was an unnecessary expense."

Fitz grinned. "There are other types of security systems. Does the church have any nosey neighbors?"

Katía smiled. "Irma Mae Jones is a bit on the nosey side, but I doubt she'd be up that time of day. She's getting up there in age. I'm not sure how much longer she'll be able to live in her home."

"Is she a church member?"

"No, but I drop in on her every now and then just to see how she's doing."

Fitz checked his watch. "It's four-thirty-seven. Want to pay her a visit before dinner?"

Katía grinned before whispering into Fitz's ear, "Not really. I'd rather have an appetizer of snuggling with you."

CHAPTER 13

The sun rose gloriously as the park pals completed their usual walk around the trail on Saturday morning. Fitz and Katía filled the others in on what they had learned yesterday.

When they returned to the lot where they had parked, Fitz noticed something on his windshield. "What's that?" he mumbled. Walking up to the car, he could tell it was a piece of paper, not a fancy flier, just a piece of white paper.

He pulled it out from under the windshield wiper, and as he read the handwritten words, a chill ran down his spine and collided with a tidal wave of anger.

"What does it say?" Katía asked.

Fitz handed her the note. It read, "BACK OFF! … OR ELSE."

Zee, Luna, and Ben had gathered to look over Katía's shoulder.

"Sounds like you've stirred up the hornets' nest," Zee said. "Who's mad at you this time?"

"I wish I knew," Fitz replied.

"I'd like to report a threatening note that was placed on my friend's car this morning." Luna had already dialed 911. When she disconnected, she said, "They're sending a deputy."

"I don't think this needed to be reported," Fitz said with a lack of conviction.

"I've heard that one before," Luna said, hands going to her hips. "Haven't you learned how much trouble we end up in when we don't report stuff like this?"

"She does have a point," Ben said.

"I didn't notice anyone comin' or goin'," Zee added. "Whoever did this is a sneaky soul."

"Do you think this is about your looking into Harley's case?" Ben asked.

"I'm sure it is," Katía answered. "What else could it be, … and what does 'or else' mean?"

"I hate to imagine," Zee said.

Fitz slipped some M&Ms into his mouth.

"I saw that," Katía said. "You're worried, too."

"OK," Fitz said. "It is concerning that someone is stealing residentially-challenged folks off the street and leaving them at crime scenes. I wish I knew who we were dealing with. A known enemy is easier to deal with than a ghost."

"You said crime scenes. Is there another one besides Harley?" Ben asked.

"Yeah, I read in the paper about a residentially-challenged man being found unconscious in someone's closet," Fitz replied.

A sheriff's car parked near where they were standing. Diann James got out and said, "You folks are going to give this park a bad name."

"We can't help it. Trouble just seems to find us," Zee replied.

"Tell me what's happened now," Diann said.

Luna explained. "We found a note on Fitz's car when we got back from our walk. Nobody saw anyone coming or going."

Katía took a photo, then held out the note, and Diann looked it over. "That's a threat, all right. Any idea who might be out to get you this time?"

"I've done a little digging into Harley Smith's case, the one where a man was found unconscious in the restaurant refrigerator. I'm assuming it's related to that."

"But that's a slam-dunk case. The man was literally caught with the cash at the scene of the crime," Diann replied.

"Except I don't believe that's what happened," Fitz said.

Diann cut him a disbelieving look. "Why would you say that?"

"Because he appears to have been knocked out while walking down the street and didn't wake up until he was in the refrigerator."

"Fitz, you know they all claim they're innocent," Diann answered.

"That's true, but I believe Harley's telling the truth. I asked the arresting officer to look into the report and see if there was enough blood or damage to the shelving that would indicate he fell and knocked himself out."

"And?" Diann asked.

"I haven't heard back from her yet."

"I see. Fitz, I believe the best idea is for you to do exactly as the note said. Leave it in the hands of the city police and lay low for a while. I'll need to keep the note as evidence," Diann said.

"Thanks for coming, Diann. Please let me know if you learn anything new about the church robbery," Katía said.

"I'll keep you updated."

Fitz tugged on his beard before asking, "Do you by any chance know the name of the man who was found unconscious in the Friedrichs' home?"

As Diann was about to get into the car, she paused. "No, I don't. I mean it, Fitz, lay low for a while. This could be serious," she said, shaking the note at him.

Fitz watched her drive off, then muttered, "Harley needs me. I can't just let it go."

"You can't seriously be considering continuing to pursue this," Katía said. "I think we should listen to Diann. I don't want to lose you before the wedding … or after, for that matter."

"Yeah, Fitz. That 'or else' has me worried," Zee added.

"Maybe you should stay at my place till the wedding. They obviously know the places you frequent," Ben suggested.

"Thanks for the concern, but I'll be wary. I'll keep my Beretta on me."

Katía put her arm around Fitz's shoulder. "You can stay at Ben's house, or I'm staying with you."

Fitz huffed, "I don't need babysitting."

"You do if you're unwilling to take a few precautions," Luna added.

Fitz popped a few more M&Ms into his mouth. "Fine, I'll stay at Ben's for a night or two."

"And not keep digging into Harley's case," Luna added.

"I try not to make promises I can't keep," Fitz replied.

"At least we made a little progress," Zee said.

"I wish the park had video surveillance," Katía groaned.

Fitz decided it was time to change the subject. "What time do you think that woman across from the church will be up?"

Katía shook her head. "Slick move, Fitz. I seldom see her light on when I get to the office, so I think she's a late sleeper. I think we should wait till after lunch." Noticing the look of confusion on the others' faces, she added, "We're going to drop in on a woman who lives across from the church and ask if she saw anything related to the robbery."

"Oh. That makes sense. Still, you be careful, Fitz," Luna said. "What if this is about the church robbery?"

"I can't see this note having anything to do with that," Fitz replied.

Fitz followed Katía to her house. He carried Buffett in rather than going through the trouble of harnessing him. As soon as he hit the floor, Buffett trotted off to greet Cotton and Snow.

They enjoyed coffee, then Katía took Fitz by the hand and led him to her bedroom.

"It's time to organize for your moving in," she announced. "Which side of the closet do you prefer?" She pulled open the folding doors to reveal a closet stuffed with clothes.

Fitz tugged his beard while he eyed the closet. Puzzled, he said, "I don't have many clothes, but I don't think they'll go in there."

"Silly, I'm going to move my summer clothes to the spare bedroom."

"I hate for you to have to do that. I can just hang mine in there."

Katía pulled Fitz into an embrace. "Fitz, I love you, and I want you to feel that this is your home. You deserve closet space and drawer space, so you're going to get it whether you like it or not." She pulled her head back and grinned. "Do you think we should let our underwear share a drawer?"

CHAPTER 14

That Saturday, while they were eating lunch, Katía said, "The note on your car has me worried."

"I think the easiest way to figure out who put the note on my car is to discover who stuck Harley in that refrigerator," Fitz answered.

"We're going to let the police tend to that, remember?"

"I think staying at Ben's is enough precaution. I can't sit back and risk Harley's being put away for something he didn't do."

Katía reached her hand across the table, and Fitz took it, bracing for another lecture about staying out of it.

"I understand. We can't just stop. I'll help any way I can."

Fitz's eyes widened. "That's not what I was expecting you to say."

"I know," she grinned.

Katía finished putting away the lunch items, and she and Fitz headed to visit the woman across from the church.

"Her name is Irma Mae Jones," Katía explained as she drove. "She lost her husband three years ago, so she's lonely.

She's also quite nosey. I see her peeking out from behind her curtains a lot when I'm coming and going from the church."

"That's just the person we need," Fitz replied. "I just hope she was spying when the church was robbed. Is she up late?"

"I don't know," Katía said. "The latest I ever leave the church is around nine, and that's rare. I have noticed her light on then, but that's not exactly late."

She pulled into Irma Mae's driveway, and they went to the door. Irma Mae answered. "Good afternoon, Pastor. Come in. You must be Fitz. I've heard a lot about you," she said while ushering them in and motioning them to sit on the paisley sofa in her living room. "It's so nice of you to drop by. It gets so lonesome here since Charlie passed. Can I get you some tea?"

Fitz started to tell her, "No thanks," but Katía responded quicker. "We'd love some. Thank you."

"Just make yourselves at home, and I'll be right back," Irma Mae said as she bustled off to the kitchen.

"I wasn't planning on being here that long," Fitz whispered.

"Hush. This will do her soul good," Katía whispered back.

Irma Mae, white hair in a poof that was tended to at the beauty parlor without fail every Thursday, returned with a tray and three iced teas.

Setting the tray on a side table, she said, "Isn't your weddin' next week? That's so excitin'. Shouldn't you be busy gettin' ready for that instead of visitin' a silly old woman like me?"

Taking the glass of tea Irma Mae offered, Katía replied, "You're not a silly old woman, Irma Mae. Quit talking like that. Actually, I think everything is ready for the wedding."

"You are an organized soul, then. Every bride I've ever known, includin' me, is pullin' their hair out the week before the weddin'."

"Our wedding is going to be right simple."

"That's nice," Irma Mae said. "I've had a lot of trouble sleepin' lately, you know? It's been gettin' harder instead of easier. Maybe I'm just gettin' too old."

Katía replied, "I'm sorry to hear that. Not sleeping well makes me feel miserable."

"Tell me about it, honey," Irma Mae responded. "I think I'm worried about whether it's time to sell the house and move into one of those places. How do you know when it's time?"

Katía answered, "I think there are two ways you'll know. One is when your daughter comes and says, 'Mom, I think it's time.'"

Irma Mae laughed. "She'd do that, too."

"The other way is when you decide you'd rather be around other people and have some help with your daily needs. You'll know when it's time. It's easy for me to tell you to stop worrying about it, but that's what you need to do. Just trust God to guide you and trust yourself to know," Katía said.

"That sounds wise. I wish I could manage to stop worryin'. That'd be nice."

Fitz sat drinking his tea and fighting the urge to go ahead and ask what he and Katía had come to find out. He fought the urge to reach for M&Ms, too.

Katía continued, "I imagine you heard about the church getting robbed."

"I sure did. That's terrible," Irma Mae replied, taking a swig of tea.

"It happened in the night or early morning on Monday. Did you happen to see a car or anything suspicious?"

"You know, I think I might have. It was one of my bad nights. I'd been up and down all night. I noticed car lights and looked out the window and saw a car parking at the church. I thought it was odd but assumed maybe someone had forgotten to turn off the heat or somethin'. I didn't connect it with the robbery."

Fitz sat up straighter. "Could you tell what kind of car it was?"

"It was one of those SUV things everybody's drivin' these days. I prefer a good ole Buick."

"Could you tell the model or the color?" Fitz asked.

"It was dark, you know. In the streetlight it looked like a darker color, maybe blue or black. I guess it could've been dark gray. I don't know what kind it was. I'm not that good with cars, you know."

Katía asked, "Do you remember what time you saw it?"

"Honey, that night was just a blur. I was up and down so much I couldn't possibly tell you. It does seem it was in the wee hours of the mornin', though."

Fitz said, "Thank you so much for sharing that. If you remember anything else, please let us know. You might be the only chance we have to catch who did this."

"Oh, my!" Irma Mae gasped. "Now I'll worry even more."

Katía tried to soothe her. "Fitz didn't mean it like that. I don't want you to worry, Irma Mae. Sometimes memories pop up when we're not trying to force them. If that happens, give me a call."

Irma Mae yawned. "Excuse me. Like I said, I haven't been sleepin' much lately."

"Fitz and I'll go so you can try for a nap," Katía said. "If you don't feel like driving to your church some Sunday, you're welcome to drop in on us."

"I might just do that one of these days."

Fitz and Katía left and once they were in the car, Fitz said, "I wish she had one of those Ring doorbells."

"That's a brilliant idea!" Katía said and pulled into the next driveway.

"What are you doing?"

"I'm checking to see if any of these other houses have video security," Katía said.

She got out, and Fitz followed. Knocking on the door drew no response. Fitz scanned the house for cameras but saw none.

"No luck here," Fitz noted.

"Let's hit the other two."

At the second house, a middle-aged man answered the door.

"Hi, I'm Katía Bancroft. I'm the pastor of the church across the street," she said, pointing.

Fitz noticed the man stiffen. *He's probably expecting her to invite him to church.*

"What can I do for you?" the man asked.

"The church was robbed in the early hours of Monday morning, and I'm checking to see if you might have a video security system."

"I'm sorry to hear about the robbery. This has always seemed like a safe area. No, we don't have that, but it sounds like it's time to invest in one."

"Thanks," Katía said.

No one was home at the last house, nor did it have visible cameras.

"It looks like we struck out," Katía said.

"Not totally," Fitz replied. "At least we know the type of vehicle that was used."

"And just how many dark SUVs are in the area?"

"True. It doesn't narrow it down much."

On the way back to Katía's house, a rare thing happened: Fitz's phone rang. He dug it out of his pocket, read the unfamiliar number, then answered the call.

"Fitz Fitzgerald, please."

"This is he."

"It's Officer Abramson. You were right. The crime scene photos show no active bleeding, and nothing seemed bent or broken. Do you have any ideas as to what really happened?"

"I do. My guess is that someone knocked Harley out and put him there as a decoy to throw suspicion off themselves. Either the restaurant owner isn't being forthcoming about what was stolen or … actually, I can't think of an or."

"Or maybe it was a scare tactic to force the owner into something?" Abramson suggested.

"I hadn't thought of that, but it's definitely a possibility," Fitz replied.

"I'm officially telling you to stay out of this, but if you learn anything else, please let me know."

"I certainly will. Oh, someone left a note on my car this morning telling me to back off."

"This is getting darker and darker. You should definitely back off, but if you don't, be careful."

"You know me too well already," Fitz said. He disconnected the call and explained to Katía what the officer had said.

"Poor Harley. This is getting serious. What do we do next?"

CHAPTER 15

Monday morning the week of the wedding dawned with a glorious array of color. As the park pals walked near the lake, the pink light reflecting off the mist hovering over the water intensified the colors. A cold breeze rattled the leaves as if they were vying for attention to their oranges, reds, and yellows.

With the exception of Saturday's visit with Irma Mae and Fitz and Katía's going to see Harley in jail on Sunday afternoon, the weekend had passed uneventfully.

"How's Harley doin'?" Zee asked.

"He seems OK. Said he's enjoying the food," Fitz chuckled.

"We've never had two cases going at once," Ben said. "Has anyone had any ideas on how to solve them?"

"All we have on the church robbery is that the burglar probably drove an SUV," Katía replied.

"That ain't much," Zee observed.

"This morning, I'm going to find Harley's lawyer and make sure she knows what Officer Abramson told me about the crime scene," Fitz added.

"You should tell the prosecuting attorney about that, too," Ben added.

"Why would we want to give them a heads up?" Fitz asked.

"So they'll realize they're prosecuting the wrong guy and drop the case," Ben answered.

"It cain't hurt to try," Zee added.

"We'll go with you, sort of as a show of force," Ben suggested.

"OK, fine. We'll find out who that is and try to talk to them, too," Fitz said.

They finished their walk, and Katía headed to the office. Luna had some chores to do, so she left, too.

"Any lawyer worth her salt won't be in the office before nine. Why don't we hit the Rabbittown Cafe for breakfast?" Ben suggested.

"Yum!" Zee said. "Let's go."

When they sat down with their plates, Zee asked, "You adjustin' to the domestic life OK?"

"Other than feeling like an imposition, it's fine," Fitz answered.

"How many times do I have to tell you, you're not an imposition," Ben said. "Snickers and I enjoy the company. It gets tiresome wandering around that house by myself."

"Well, thanks for putting up with me. I'd never hear the end of it if I didn't stay with you," Fitz said.

"You'll never hear the end of it from me if you don't stop moping about being an imposition," Ben laughed. "Where's that lawyer's office?"

"I don't know yet," Fitz said while carefully wrapping a piece of bacon in a napkin.

"That's a good idea," Zee said. "We should take the pooches a piece, too." He and Ben followed Fitz's lead and dutifully wrapped bacon for King and Snickers.

Ben fished his phone from his pocket. "What's that lawyer's name, and I'll look up her office?"

"I believe Harley said it was Lauren Hamilton," Fitz answered.

Ben typed the name into the search bar. "Whew, hoity toity! I expected her to be in a dingy office in some low rent building."

"Where is it?" Zee asked.

"She's in one of the old mansions on Green Street," Ben replied.

"I've always wanted to go in one of those places," Zee said.

"Looks like today's your lucky day," Ben said. "Parking might be tight. Why don't we take my car, and I'll bring you back afterward?"

They entered the antebellum home that had been immaculately preserved. "Don't drool on the rug," Ben whispered to Zee.

"This place is gorgeous," Zee said.

Fitz located the lawyer's office on a directory. "It's on the second floor."

"I don't care how much my knee hurts, I'm goin' up these amazin' stairs," Zee said and started a slow climb, hanging tightly to the walnut rail of the formal staircase. "Up with the good. Up with the good."

Fitz shook his head and followed. "You beat anything I've ever seen."

"This is probably my only chance to climb anything this fancy," Zee replied.

Fitz passed Zee at the top of the stairs and located the door to Hamilton's office at the end of the hall.

"I bet this used to be a bedroom," Ben observed.

Fitz knocked on the door, which made him feel silly. *This is an office. I should just walk in.*

A young woman, blond and thin, opened the door with a puzzled expression. "Come on in," she said. "I'm Gina. How can I help you?"

"I'd like to speak to Lauren Hamilton about a friend she is representing," Fitz explained.

"I don't remember seeing you on her calendar this morning. Do you have an appointment?" Gina asked.

"No, but this is important," Fitz replied. "I've discovered some evidence that she needs to be aware of."

The door at the back of the tiny reception area opened, and Lauren walked out. "It's OK, Gina. I'll listen to what he—they have to say," she said. "Come on in."

She led them into a meticulously organized room. Her desk had one file, a laptop, and a photo of what Fitz presumed to be her husband and daughter. He appreciated the organization.

"The walls were built before insulation, so I couldn't help hearing. What have you uncovered regarding Harley's case?"

"How'd you know we were here about Harley?" Zee asked.

"Because Mr. Fitzgerald chased me down in the parking lot the other day." She turned her focus back to Fitz. "Well?"

"The arresting officer took another look at the crime scene photos. She said there was no sign of active bleeding, and nothing in the refrigerator was bent or damaged like it should have been had Harley tripped and fallen."

Lauren opened the file on her desk and pulled out some photos. "I just happen to be working on his case now." She looked over the photos. "You're right. There isn't a pool of blood. It does look like he might have been knocked out and placed in there. I hadn't noticed that." She continued to pore over the photos, then looked up as if she had forgotten the three men were there.

"Thank you for bringing this to my attention. Is there anything else?" she asked.

"I'd like to know who the prosecuting attorney is," Fitz asked.

"Why is that?" she asked, her blue eyes narrowing.

"I want to see if I can talk them into dropping this case," Fitz answered.

He waited while she eyed him. Finally, she said, "It might be better if I ambush him with this information during the trial."

"It will be better for Harley if the case is just thrown out," Fitz countered with a tug to his beard.

"OK. The attorney's name is Warren Windsor. He might not be as easy to get to as me."

"Thanks. If I can do anything else to help with the case, let me know," Fitz said.

Lauren replied, "I will, and I appreciate your bringing this to my attention. Please let me know if you uncover anything else of importance."

"I will."

The three men exited the office. Zee wanted to go back down the stairs, so they followed him. Once outside, Zee said, "That was one skinny woman. She needs to eat more."

Fitz and Ben laughed. "Shall we track down this Warren Windsor?" Ben asked.

"There's no time like the present," Zee replied.

Once in the car, Ben did a search for the attorney's office, then drove there, parking in the deck near the courthouse.

"We'll have to leave any pocketknives or other dangerous weapons in the car," Fitz said. They checked their pockets before heading inside and making it through security successfully. After locating the office, Fitz led the way in.

"Can I help you?" A stern-looking woman asked.

"We'd like to speak with Mr. Windsor, please," Fitz said.

When woman stood, Fitz was afraid she was going to grab him by the collar and toss him out the door. "Mr. Windsor doesn't see people without an appointment," she announced, glaring as though she expected them to understand that was their invitation to leave.

"I understand, but this is regarding a case he is prosecuting. He might decide not to proceed once he hears what I have to say," Fitz said, giving his beard a tug and forcing himself not to go for M&Ms.

"Well, Mr. Windsor is in court right now."

"Could I leave him a message?" Fitz asked.

The woman stood erect, waiting.

"I need a pen and paper," Fitz added.

After a long pause, she plopped a pen and a legal pad onto the corner of the desk and sat back down.

Fitz wrote, explaining what the crime scene photos revealed and his suspicions about Harley's being planted as a decoy. He ended with a recommendation that Winston consider dropping the case. He added his name and number, then returned the pen and pad to the corner of her desk.

She didn't look up from her computer, so Fitz said, "Please see that Mr. Windsor gets that." He led the others out of the office.

"That woman has ice in her veins," Zee quipped.

"I hope the attorney sees the wisdom in your note," Ben said.

"I hope she doesn't wad it up and throw it away," Fitz added.

CHAPTER 16

Tuesday morning at the park, Fitz heard a car door shut just as he was finishing washing up. *Zee's here early.* He put on deodorant, buttoned his shirt, pulled on his coat, and went outside.

"Good morning!" Katía chirped. "I think the sunrise is going to be extra gorgeous today, so I want to make sure I catch it on camera."

"I was expecting Zee," Fitz said, surprised to find Katía there this early.

"Sorry to disappoint you," Katía chuckled.

"It's no disappointment," Fitz said, coming in for a hug and kiss.

Keeping her arms around his neck, she said, "In a few days we can wake up side by side, then ride to the park together. I'm looking forward to that."

"Me, too," Fitz replied, imagining what it would be like to wake up in the house next to her.

Zee pulled up while they were hugging. Opening the door, he said, "That's a beautiful sight. Lovebirds in action."

"Morning, Zee," Fitz said.

Katía echoed Fitz's greeting while Zee moaned and groaned to stand up.

"This cooler weather's wreakin' havoc on my ole joints," he said, handing King's leash to Fitz.

"I'm going to get set up so I'm ready for the first hint of light," Katía announced, pulling her camera and tripod from her Prius. "Just stay and visit with the others, Fitz. I'll be setting up and concentrating on the shots anyway." With that she was off.

"Should I go with her?" Fitz asked Zee when he came back out.

"Naw, man. She told you to stay here. Don't try to read anythin' into it. I think she was plain as day."

Ben and Luna pulled up together. "Where's Katía?" Luna asked, sounding worried as she got out of her car.

"She went to set up her camera," Fitz said, pointing to her dark shape that he could barely still see.

"Good. I was worried when I saw her car but not her," Luna replied.

"What are you worried about?" Ben asked.

"Fitz did get that threat on his car the other day, remember?" she replied.

"I see. You thought someone might have nabbed her to get at him," Ben said.

"With the dangers we've faced this year, don't you think it makes sense to worry?" Luna added.

"I sure do, but so far so good," Ben replied.

"Y'all quit thinkin' such negative thoughts. Let's go for a walk and enjoy another beautiful fall day," Zee said.

With Buffett, Snickers, and King leashed up, they headed to the trail.

"There comes Katía's picture," Zee said, pointing to the faint hint of coral in the east. By the time they got around to where Katía had set up her camera, the light was putting on a show. Mist hung over the water in the cold air, creating an eerie dimension to the scene.

"This is incredible," Katía said, not taking her eye off the camera as she made some adjustments. "Y'all keep going. I'm too busy to talk."

The group made it a little farther down the trail when the sound of breaking glass shattered the tranquil morning.

"Someone's breaking into a car," Fitz said and led the way along the side of a ball field to get to the cars as quickly as possible.

"Y'all go on. I'll get there when I can," Zee called as he lagged behind.

When Fitz topped the hill enough to see the cars, he saw taillights headed out of the park and Katía aiming her camera in that direction. He, Ben, and Luna rushed up to Katía.

"Which car?" Ben asked.

"Looks like it was mine," Fitz replied, walking over to assess the damage and see what was stolen. The driver's side front window was shattered, pieces of glass littering the front seat. Fitz opened the door and surveyed his belongings.

"Everything seems to be in place. That's odd." At that moment he noticed a large rock lying on the passenger floorboard. "What's that?" he asked, walking around the car to retrieve the rock. The others gathered around to see.

Fitz found a string duct-taped to the rock, and on the end of the string was a note: "I told you to back off. Now look what you made me do. Your bride-to-be will be next."

"And you wondered why I was worried earlier," Luna said.

When Zee walked up, Ben filled him in on what they had found. Luna had already dialed 911 while Fitz was still examining the note.

"It's gonna be a cold ride this mornin'," Zee observed.

"They're sending a deputy … again," Luna said after disconnecting the call.

Fitz shuddered as rage ran rampant through his body. Katía moved her camera so it hung on her back and embraced Fitz from behind. "It's going to be OK. We'll protect each other," she said.

Fitz patted her forearm, her closeness calming him.

"Katía, I think you should consider staying at my house, too," Ben offered. "This is getting scary."

"What made them attack a second time?" Fitz wondered. He held to Katía's arms, lost in thought.

"We don't need this right before your wedding," Luna added.

"I went to see the two lawyers yesterday. I bet one of them told whoever is behind this," Fitz muttered.

"You think one of the attorneys ratted you out?" Zee asked. "That don't seem legal."

A sheriff's car parked nearby, and Diann James got out. "Talk about déjà vu," she said, walking up to the group. "What's going on this time?" Snickers wandered over to sniff, and Diann patted her on the head.

Fitz held the rock out. "Someone didn't like my car window."

"I see," she said, eyeing the broken window. "Let me guess: This happened while you were walking and no one saw who did it, just like last time."

"Oh, I forgot to check my pictures," Katía said, pulling her camera up to see the images she had taken as the car sped out of the park. She scanned the three shots she had gotten. "It was still pretty dark. Let me zoom in on this one. … Great. They had their license plate covered with something. I can tell it was an SUV … maybe a BMW."

"That's an uptown crook," Zee said.

"Do you mind if I see the photos?" Diann asked.

"Of course not. I'm happy to send them to you, too," Katía replied, handing Diann the camera.

"You're right. It does look like a BMW, and the tag is definitely covered with something. Whoever did this was either being extra careful, or they knew you are a photographer," Diann said.

"That's creepy," Ben said. "How could they know that much about her?"

"Social media is a gold mine for criminals. They can learn tons of info about their targets just by looking through posts," Diann replied. "Of course, that doesn't apply to Fitz. You haven't gotten into social media, have you?"

"Not at all," Fitz replied, popping five M&Ms into his mouth. "We have to protect Katía. I want these people caught before they can get to her."

"Based on the note, I think the best thing you can do is leave Harley's case alone … at least I'm assuming that's what this is related to. Any idea what provoked this rock to jump through your window?"

"I talked to Harley's lawyer and the prosecuting attorney yesterday," Fitz said.

"I see. Anything stolen from your car?"

"Not that I can tell. Wait! I didn't check the back." Keeping his body between Diann and the car, Fitz opened the lockbox to find all three of his extra Berettas in place. "No, it looks like everything's here."

Diann tucked her notepad away. "So your theory is that someone knocked out this Harley guy and left him in the restaurant so he'd get the blame for whatever this person stole, even though as far as we know nothing is missing. Is that right?"

"That sums it up. I think someone is after something the councilman has … or had," Fitz replied.

"I see. Please text or email me the photos," Diann said, handing Katía her card. "We'll coordinate with Gainesville City on this investigation. I'll get the crime lab to see if they can enhance the photos enough to give us better information."

"I'll see what I can do with them, too," Katía said.

"Fitz, I mean it, stay away from this case … if not for your sake, then for Katía's."

CHAPTER 17

After Deputy James left, the park pals gathered at a picnic table under the pavilion, everyone sitting as if the weight of the morning's event was pushing them down. Fitz popped M&Ms into his mouth and tugged his beard. Katía rubbed his shoulder.

Fitz's heart and mind were at war. *I have two impossible situations. I can't risk Katía getting hurt … or worse. She nearly died in that cave last summer. But if I back off, Harley could go to prison for something he didn't do. I can't let that happen either. I can't live with myself if either of those things happens. Someone must be watching me to know that I'm still trying to figure out what's going on.* Finally, a voice seeped through the tornado in his soul.

"Hey, space cadet." It was Ben. Fitz looked at Ben, bewildered, having been so caught up in his thoughts.

Having Fitz's attention, Ben said, "We have to keep Katía safe, Fitz. You can't keep digging into this case."

"I don't know if I could live with myself if Harley goes to jail, though."

"You can't keep digging, but we can," Ben grinned. "Just help us figure out what to do next."

"I can't ask you to do that. It's too dangerous," Fitz said.

"True. We'll have to be discreet," Luna added. "What would you do next?"

Fitz tugged his beard and popped more M&Ms into his mouth as he pondered what his next step might be.

"A better question might be what prompted someone to throw a rock through your window this mornin'?" Zee added. "If we figure that out, it might lead us to a trail worth followin'."

Fitz's mind shifted gears. "My best guess is that someone is following me."

"Could be one of them lawyers is rattin' you out," Zee suggested.

"Why would a lawyer do that?" Katía asked.

"That does seem odd," Luna said.

"It don't if one of 'em has their hands in the devil's pocket," Zee suggested.

"That's a scary thought," Luna said. "I'd think it would have to be somebody with deep pockets to bribe a lawyer."

"Unless they had something on the lawyer," Ben added.

"This is startin' to sound like a movie," Zee quipped.

Ben laughed. "That gives me an idea. We should write up the things we've been through and turn them into a movie … or at least a book."

"You should work on that in your spare time," Katía said.

"I think we're getting sidetracked," Luna pointed out. "I have no idea how we find out if someone is bribing a lawyer, much less who that someone is."

"Which of the lawyers do you think is the most likely culprit?" Ben asked.

Fitz grinned. "The best way might be to take the direct approach."

"What's that?" Zee asked.

"Instead of trying to figure out which lawyer and who's bribing them, we could set a trap for the thug that threw the rock. If we catch him, we'll know who's behind it. The rest should be easy," Fitz suggested.

"Oh, no," Zee said. "That don't sound good."

"How would we set a trap when we don't even know whom we're trapping?" Ben asked.

"We know where they like to strike," Fitz observed. "I can go back to the two lawyers today, and we'll lie in wait for them tomorrow morning."

"What if they attack Katía at home tonight?" Luna asked.

A cold chill oozed down Fitz's spine at the thought.

"I think you should stay at my house for a while," Ben suggested again.

"Or our house. Carlos and I would love the company. You can bring the cats."

"I don't know what to say," Katía said. "I don't want to let these creeps run me out of my home. I have a gun, and they're coming to install a security system today. I think I'll be all right."

"Good grief," Zee moaned. "Stubbornness ain't a virtue, you know."

Fitz chuckled at the look Katía shot Zee. "I'll park in your driveway tonight. That will double the protection."

"That's sweet of you, Fitz, but if any of the church folks pass by, they will assume you're in bed with me," Katía replied.

Fitz felt his face flush. "Oh." He popped M&Ms into his mouth. "If you refuse to go to Luna's or Ben's, then pick me up after dark and smuggle me in. I'll sleep on the couch. I can't bear to risk your getting attacked."

"Ugh! Y'all are impossible. I'll be all right. It's Fitz we really need to worry about."

"I already have litter set up," Ben added with a grin.

Katía shot Ben the same withering look she had given Zee. "I'll think about it, but now I have to get ready for a meeting about the new shelter." She got into her car and left.

"I don't think she's happy about our suggestions," Zee observed.

"Don't you guys let her stay alone tonight. I have to get ready for an appointment." Luna took off, too.

"Why didn't I think of this before? I need to find out who the other guy is, the one they found in that closet, and pay him a visit. I'll bet he tells the same tale as Harley," Fitz said.

"You mean Zee and I should pay this guy a visit," Ben corrected. "You're staying out of it, remember?"

"They've made two threats. If they were serious about doing something, they would have acted on the 'or else' this time," Fitz replied.

"I hope all the 'or else' meant was the rock through your window," Ben said.

"Better safe than sorry," Zee suggested. "Do you think your old buddy, Geraldine, could find the guy's name?"

"I bet she could." Fitz checked his watch. "She might be in by now." He dialed the sheriff's office and asked for Geraldine.

"Hey, Geraldine, it's Fitz."

"Hey, Fitz. It's been a while. I assume this is trouble like usual."

"No trouble. I just want to get the name of the man they arrested for breaking into the Friedrichs' home.

"Are you sure this isn't trouble because it sure smells like it? I saw the issue with the note on your car."

"Just trying to keep innocent folks out of prison, Geraldine. Please look up his name and see if he posted bail."

"Well, since you said please, give me a second. … It was Nate Powell, and it shows that he's still in jail. Let me guess, you want me to transfer the call so you can set up a visit."

"You're the best," Fitz said. He was able to arrange for Ben and Zee to see Nate at 11:00am that morning.

"Who is it?" Zee asked as soon as Fitz disconnected.

"Nate Powell."

"I know him. Used to have a tent near his before I got my car. Nice guy," Zee replied.

Ben asked, "Hey, Fitz, do you want the name of that windshield repair company I used last spring? They did a good job, and they'll come to you to do it."

"Sure."

While Ben looked up the number, he said, "Y'all are welcome to come to the house while we wait to go see this Nate guy."

"Sounds good to me," Zee said.

When 10:15 a.m. rolled around, Ben and Zee left for the jail, armed with a list of questions they wanted answers to. Fitz stayed behind to wait for the windshield repair company to show up.

Being alone in Ben's house stirred odd feelings. He sat on the couch with Buffett in his lap and Snickers and King napping nearby. He lay his head back to let the swirl of emotions take form and emerge into consciousness.

The first to emerge was warm. Katía. Next came a dark fog. It took shape as fear. *Katía is in danger. I'm in danger. Am I putting Ben and Zee in danger, too?* He continued to sit and wait. A third form emerged: Anger. It sat heavy and unpleasant on his heart. *Why are they doing this to residentially-challenged folks? Why pick on us? Do they consider us expendable or just easy targets? How did they know the people they were grabbing were unhoused? Did they know, or did it just happen that way?*

There was something else hesitant to take shape, bubbling up from down deep. When it finally formed, it was a rockslide. Change. *My life is changing drastically. I'm in love. I'm no longer alone. I'm about to be housed. Why does that worry me? I should be relieved.*

A knock on the door startled Fitz, prompting Buffett to jump down and the dogs to bark. Fitz opened the door to find a man from the windshield repair company standing there. His name tag read, "Joe." Still in a fog from being so deep in thought, Fitz took a moment to realize he needed to show him the car. Leading Joe to his car, Fitz explained, "Somehow a rock or something hit the driver's door window. It will need to be replaced."

Joe scrunched up his face. "I just cain't 'magine how that could've happened. I bet someone threw somethin' at it. Didn't you find a brick or somethin' inside?"

"I did find a rock," Fitz said, not wanting to fully explain and hoping that would satisfy him.

"OK, I'll get on it. Should take 'bout thirty minutes to an hour. I'll knock when I'm done."

Fitz took that as a recommendation to go inside and wait … to wait for him to finish the job, to wait for Ben and Zee to get back, to wait for the wedding, to wait for the big changes coming to his life.

CHAPTER 18

Katía arrived early for the shelter meeting. Not being sure how to navigate the Vine and Branches church facility to find the meeting room, she decided to enter at the door marked, "Office."

Opening the door, she heard voices down the hall. *This isn't going to be hard.* She walked into a room that looked like it was laid out for a Sunday school class. Three other pastors were chatting.

"Hey, Katía, and welcome," Charis Stanton said, her green eyes smiling as much as her lips.

"Hey, Charis, it's good to see you."

"Have the police made any progress on the robbery at your church?" Charis asked.

"Not yet. The deputy said there wasn't enough evidence left behind, so it's unlikely they'll ever catch the crook."

"I'm sorry about that. I think a lot of robberies are never solved," Charis said as a few other pastors and a couple of lay people trickled in.

"True, and it's infuriating," Katía replied. "A day late and a dollar short, but our church is discussing a security system now."

Charis checked her watch. "Oooh! We'd better get started." She invited everyone to have a seat around the tables, which were arranged in a square. "This is the closest I could come to a round table." The group laughed as they took their seats.

"Let's begin with a word of prayer," Charis said, bowing her head. "Dear loving Lord, you created each human being on this planet and gently breathed into us the breath of your Spirit. Please guide us as we seek to plan a new shelter to help care for your creations who are struggling to care for themselves. Give us insight, courage, and direction. In Jesus' name we pray. Amen."

She looked up and continued. "We have a couple of new faces with us today, so some introductions are in order."

Roger O'Brien, the Presbyterian pastor introduced Trevor Middleton, a building contractor who had volunteered to help with planning details. He was a heavy-muscled man with short blond hair and green eyes.

Next, Ansel Anderson, the Catholic Priest, introduced a man with bushy black hair, thick-rimmed black glasses, and intense brown eyes named David Ralston. He was an architect who had volunteered to draw up the plans for the shelter.

With the introductions out of the way, Charis said, "OK, let's talk turkey. Sorry, I couldn't resist with Thanksgiving just a few weeks away. Our first item is to list any ideas we've had for naming the shelter. Let's write them down and let them bake for a while to see which one rises up as the leader."

"Do we need to get you a snack?" Katía chuckled.

"I'm on a roll, aren't I?" Charis replied. The group laughed again. "OK, did anyone have any inspiration for a name?"

Alister Bates of St. Peter's Baptist spoke up. "The name 'Heaven's Door' came to my mind."

Charis got up to write it down on the whiteboard. "I can see that. It's a doorway to a new life."

"It might have too many connotations of death, though," Jim Hamilton of First Baptist commented.

Charis said, "Let's try not to discuss right now. Let's just get the ideas down." She wrote the others as they came up: New Roots, The Shepherd's House, My Place, and Hope House. For her idea, Katía went with something Zee had suggested: "The Launching Pad."

Charis continued with the agenda. "If there are no others, we'll let those stew while we move on to the bad news. I just got word from Councilwoman Jenkins that there is a proposal being brought forward to consider cutting funding for the shelter director from the city's budget. Obviously, that will seriously impact our plans."

"Let me guess whose idea that was," Katía said, trying to quell the surge of anger that plowed through her heart.

"She didn't say who was bringing the proposal," Charis replied.

"I'm sure it's Winslow Johnston. He's been trying to defeat this shelter from the get-go," Katía added.

"You can say that again," Carmen Sánchez said.

"I will assume you're correct," Charis said. "The question is, what can we do about it?"

Pastor Olster said, "We could start a letter-writing campaign by asking people in our congregations to write letters to the council members stating how much this shelter is needed for the community, the positive impacts it will have, and voicing their support for the project."

"Maybe even add a reminder that they are voters," Alister added.

"We could write up a list of the positive impacts we expect the shelter to have for the city to provide. That would make it easier for the folks writing letters," Ansel suggested.

"Good idea, Ansel," Charis replied. "I'll be happy to put together the list if all of you will email your ideas.

"We need to find out when this proposal will be discussed and rally the community to show up again," Carmen added.

"I agree," Katía said. "I don't want to take any chances. In the meantime, I think I'll have a talk with our problem child since he's a member of my flock."

The meeting concluded after a discussion of the services people would like to see the shelter offer and the types of spaces that would be needed to do that.

As people were saying their goodbyes, Charis came up to Katía. "Are you sure you want to approach Councilman Johnston on this? I'd hate for you to stir up a hornets' nest in your church."

"I just can't imagine why he's so against the shelter," Katía replied.

"He might still be after the property," Charis suggested.

"That's probably it, but I sense this goes deeper than that."

"Well, I wish you luck. If you'd like me to come with you, just let me know. Either way, it would probably be a good idea to let your anger simmer down before you talk with him."

"You're right," Katía said.

She left the meeting and drove straight to The Oasis, lucking up and finding a parking spot on the square rather than having to go to the deck. Feeling the need for some moral support before facing Winslow, she called Fitz. It was 10:52 a.m.

"Hey, Fitz. What are you up to?"

"I'm at Ben's. What are you up to?"

"I'm parked near The Oasis. Winslow is bringing a proposal to strip funding for the shelter director's salary from the city budget. I'm working on getting myself calmed down enough to talk to him about it."

"Oh, dear. Do you think talking to him is a good idea?"

"Somebody has to. I want to find out why he is so against this shelter. I'm beginning to think there's more to it than wanting that piece of property."

"I bet he's just trying everything he can to get his hands on it. A restaurant there would make him a lot of money."

"Maybe you're right. Still, I think I'll go in and tell him how much that money means to the success of the shelter."

"OK, but choose your words carefully. He is a church member, and I'm sure he could stir up lots of trouble for you."

Katía walked up to the restaurant just as a waiter was turning the sign from Closed to Open. As she walked in, the hostess asked, "How many in your party?" as she pulled menus from the counter.

"I'm not eating. I'm here to see Mr. Johnston."

"Oh," the young lady said. "I think he's in the refrigerator inventorying supplies. I'll see if he's available." She hurried off, leaving Katía waiting near the door.

"Hello, Pastor," Winslow said, walking out the kitchen door in a coat. "What brings you in?"

A strategy flashed into Katía's mind all of a sudden, and she decided to go with it. "I heard someone is going to bring a proposal to cut the money for the new shelter director's salary from the city budget. I wanted to see if we could count on you to vote against that. Even though it's just part of the salary, the money will go a long way in helping the shelter succeed."

Katía had trouble reading the expression on Winslow's face. He chuckled and said, "Pastor, I believe you suspect I am the one bringing that proposal, and that is true. I have no intention of voting against it." His eyes hardened as he spoke.

"I don't understand why you are so opposed to this new shelter."

"Because another shelter is the last thing this city needs. Now if you'll excuse me, I have work to get done before the lunch crowd." He stomped back through the kitchen door.

CHAPTER 19

itz heard Ben's garage door opening and checked his watch. It read: 11:53 a.m. *That was quick.* He slid to the edge of the couch, prompting Buffett to jump out of his lap. "Sorry, Bud."

Ben led Zee inside, and Fitz asked, "Well?"

"You were right. He said he was walking back to his tent when a car stopped, and two men jumped out. The next thing he knew, the police were waking him up in a closet," Ben reported.

"This is just odd," Fitz said. "Geraldine said nothing was reported stolen in his case, either."

"There's somethin' rotten in Denmark," Zee observed.

"Yeah, and it stinks all the way over here," Ben added.

"There has to be a connection between these two incidents," Fitz said, popping a few M&Ms into his mouth.

"How come you're not as fat as a hog, eatin' all those M&Ms?" Zee asked.

"High metabolism, I guess," Fitz replied, his mind scrambling around the two cases. "We need to find out if there's a connection between Winslow Johnston and the Friedrichs."

"That's a good thing to put Luna to work on," Ben said.

Fitz scrunched his eyes and tugged his beard.

"She's good at chasing things down on social media. That could give us the connection," Ben explained, pulling out his phone.

While Ben talked to Luna, Fitz wondered why someone would want to place Harley and Nate at crime scenes where apparently no crime occurred. *It just doesn't make sense. Something had to be stolen that they're not telling us about* … "Or photographed," he muttered.

"What do you mean, 'or photographed?'" Zee asked.

"What if they were photographing documents rather than stealing?"

"Why wouldn't they just snatch 'em?" Zee asked.

"Because they didn't want it known they had the information, maybe?" Fitz suggested.

"Like recipes from The Oasis?" Zee asked.

"That could be a possibility. If this other guy turns out to own a restaurant, that will make it more likely. It could be someone wanting to open a restaurant and looking to get recipes to give themselves a good start."

"Seems like a mighty hard way to get a recipe," Zee said.

"You're right. It has to be something else," Fitz replied.

"If I went to the trouble of breaking into somebody's house, I'd want to get something good for it," Zee added.

"You're right again. What if they both had a stash of drugs?" Fitz asked.

"I wouldn't tell the police my drugs were stolen," Zee observed.

"Luna's working on it and will let us know if she finds anything," Ben said, joining the conversation. "It sounds like you two about have this case solved."

"Johnston seems like a jerk, but I don't see him as a drug dealer," Fitz said.

"Maybe he keeps a personal stash, and the burglar knew about it. Druggies will go to any length for that next hit. A guy broke into my parents' condo in the middle of the night, went into the bedroom, and stole Dad's wallet while they were asleep. They didn't even know anyone had been there till the next morning when they found the back door open and the wallet missing," Ben said.

"But I don't think a druggie would go to the trouble of knocking someone out and dragging them to the scene of the crime," Fitz replied.

"Unless they were crazed out of their minds," Zee said.

Fitz smoothed his beard. "Still, my hunch tells me this is bigger."

A knock on the front door preceded its flying open and Katía's storming in. "That is one infuriating man! He wouldn't even talk to me about his proposal to withdraw funding from the shelter. Just said the shelter was the last thing Gainesville needs. Well, I think it's a big need!"

Fitz, Ben, and Zee stood with mouths open. "I don't believe I've ever seen you so worked up. What did he do?"

"He just said the shelter is the last thing the city needs and walked back to the kitchen," Katía replied. "Make sure y'all write letters to all the council members, even him, to voice your opinion on the matter."

"Where's a piece of paper, and I'll start right now?" Zee said, rubbing his hands together.

Ben pulled a few pieces of paper out of the printer and handed them over. "Don't put who it's to, and we'll make copies to save some writing."

"Brilliant," Zee said, sitting down at the counter.

"Could Johnston be into drugs?" Fitz asked Katía.

"I don't think so, but he might need some if I get ahold of him," she answered.

Ben's phone rang. "I'm going to put you on speaker, Luna."

"Hey, guys! It looks like the Friedrichs and Johnstons are good friends. I found several posts showing the four of them doing things together. The Friedrichs own an Italian restaurant in Flowery Branch, so they have that in common, too," Luna reported.

"So these two ... incidents weren't random break-ins. They're connected someway," Ben observed.

"I'm sure it was the same perpetrators since they did both burglaries the same way," Fitz added.

"I'm off to have lunch with a friend," Luna chimed in. "Let me know if you want me to look up anything else."

Ben disconnected the call, then added, "I still don't get why they would go to the trouble of framing these two guys. It would have been so much easier just to break in, do whatever it is they did, and leave."

"That don't make much sense. On the other hand, when Luna mentioned lunch, my stomach took notice," Zee said.

"I'm not sure I have enough sandwich fixings for everybody," Ben said.

"I could run to the Subway," Fitz offered.

"That sounds good to me," Katía replied. "Everybody enter what you want on your sandwich in the app, and we'll go pick them up." She passed her phone to Ben.

Fitz told Buffett to stay and visit, and he and Katía left to pick up the sandwiches. The sandwich artist was building the last one when they arrived. While waiting, an idea struck Fitz.

"I need to make sure both Nate's and Harley's lawyers know about the other's case," he said.

"Do you think that will do any good?" Katía asked.

"They'll know to be looking for a pattern and realize how unlikely it is that two people could commit a burglary and knock themselves out within a few days of each other."

Back at Ben's house, Fitz tracked down the lawyer representing Nate and gave him a call, explaining the similarities between the two cases. When he started to call

Harley's lawyer, Ben said, "You should let me make that call. You're staying out of this, remember?"

"There's no point in both of us being on their radar," Fitz replied before placing the call.

"You're on a roll," Zee said when Fitz disconnected the call. "Ya reckon it would do any good to make sure the prosecuting attorneys know, too?"

"That's a good idea, Zee," Ben said.

After discovering the prosecuting attorney was the same man for both cases, Fitz said, "I think I'll try dropping in on Mr. Windsor again. Maybe I'll catch him this time."

"Good grief! You don't seem to understand what staying out of a case means," Ben said.

"I'm not letting Harley and Nate get put away for something they didn't do, nor am I interested in putting you in the crosshairs. I think it should be me who goes. That'll keep your house off their radar."

"What was the point of Zee and me going to see Nate, then?" Ben countered.

"I shouldn't have let you do that either," Fitz said.

"Not to change the subject, but Katía, you didn't come in with any bags," Ben observed. "I hope you're still planning to stay here tonight."

"I really appreciate the offer, but I've decided to stay at home. I'll sleep better there, and I don't need to wear myself out before Saturday."

Fitz tugged at his beard, then reached into his pocket to discover he was out of M&Ms.

Katía, apparently noticing Fitz's forlorn expression, asked, "What?"

"I'm out of M&Ms."

"Is that all? I thought you were going to argue with me about staying at home."

"I am, and the M&Ms would have given me strength," Fitz said. "You'll sleep a lot better here than you will if someone breaks in and nabs you."

"Nobody's going to break in. You said yourself that it was an empty threat," Katía replied, hands on her hips.

Fitz stood and embraced her. "I'll sleep better if I know you're safe."

"You cain't argue with that. You don't want ole Fitz showin' up at your weddin' all baggy-eyed and yawnin'," Zee said.

"Good grief! All right, I'll stay here tonight, but I'd better not be coming into a house full of snoring old men."

CHAPTER 20

As Fitz walked along the sidewalk toward the prosecuting attorney's office, he passed two men talking. They shook hands, and he heard one of them say, "Warren, it's been good having lunch and catching up with you. We'll have to do this again soon."

Fitz stopped a few steps away and waited for them to finish their conversation before approaching the one named Warren. "Warren Windsor?" he asked.

The man stopped, eyes narrowing. "Yes?"

"I'm Fitz Fitzgerald, and I wanted to point out an important detail about two cases you are prosecuting."

"I'm sorry. I can't discuss ongoing cases, especially not with riffraff like you."

Swallowing his anger, Fitz replied, "The lives of two innocent men are in your hands. I'd think you'd at least take a second to hear what I have to say."

Warren rolled his eyes, checked his watch, and said, "Your second is about up."

"The two cases involve residentially-challenged men. One was found unconscious in a restaurant refrigerator and the other in a closet."

"So?"

"Doesn't it seem highly unlikely that two people could have knocked themselves out while trying to commit robberies in such a short span of time?"

"Look, these are easy convictions. They were caught red-handed." He turned and walked toward the building.

Fitz called out, "There is something bigger going on here. Those two men were abducted and planted at the scenes."

Warren stopped but didn't turn around. Fitz continued, "These crimes are about something more dangerous than attempted robbery. If you don't recognize that, you'll be part of the problem."

Warren walked on, leaving Fitz fuming. He walked back to the car, muttering, "He could at least have the decency to hear me out."

Sitting down in the car, he felt the sting of Warren's name-calling. *Riffraff.* Looking in the mirror, he wondered, "Is it the beard? Maybe I should get cleaned up before the wedding." He ran his hand through the beard and his long, graying hair. *I wonder what I'd look like with a haircut and beard trim.*

He drove back to Ben's, pondering the idea of improving his appearance for the wedding. He walked into the house, and Buffett greeted him with meows and leg rubs. Bending down, he petted the cat. "I missed you, too." He found Ben at the computer, and Zee asleep on the couch.

"How'd it go?" Ben asked.

"He called me riffraff and didn't want to talk. I told him anyway."

"The dirtbag," Ben replied.

"It got me to wondering. Do you think I should get a haircut and trim up my beard before the wedding? Make myself more presentable?"

Still lying on the couch, Zee answered, "You could use a little tidyin'."

Fitz looked at Ben, who nodded his head. "It wouldn't be a bad idea unless you just want to make a statement. But I recommend asking Katía before you do anything. She might prefer you the way you are."

"You're right. I'll ask her at supper tonight. We're planning to eat at her house, then come over here."

Fitz left Ben's in time to arrive at Katía's house by 4:30 p.m. so she wouldn't be there alone, stopping to fill up with gas on the way. When he got back into the car, he said to Buffett, "Do you remember this place? This is where I nearly went back to drinking last winter. You saved me again."

Buffett rubbed his chin, and Fitz said, "You're my miracle cat. I'd probably be dead by now if it weren't for you." After a few more chin rubs and purring, Fitz started the vehicle and drove to Katía's. He took in his Beretta just in case.

When Katía walked through the door, she called, "Close your eyes! I have my dress." She hurried to the bedroom to hang it up.

Coming back to the kitchen, she set her purse on the table and sighed. "I've been sending out emails most of the afternoon to drum up a response to that weasel's proposal. It was such an unnecessary waste of time. Why can't he just cooperate with the rest of the community? Losing our offering money is going to be even more serious if the city pulls their part of the funding."

Fitz hugged her and said, "I'm sorry you had a rough day. It's a shame to have lost that thirty-six hundred dollars."

Katía pulled back, eyes wide. "What do you mean, thirty-six hundred dollars? No one knew how much was in the offering box."

"That's how much Johnston said was stolen on one of his radio broadcasts."

"Why would he say that? Did he just make it up?"

Fitz pulled his beard. "Maybe he wanted to make it sound like a serious crime."

Katía shook her head. "I guess he'll say anything to manipulate people. I'm really struggling to love him like Jesus said I should."

"I don't blame you."

"How did your afternoon go?"

"I got called riffraff."

Katía pulled him in for another hug. "I'm sorry. Who would say such a thing about my future husband?"

"The prosecuting attorney. He wasn't interested in what I had to say about the cases."

"It sounds like we both have goats to contend with," Katía said.

"He did get me to thinking, and Ben said I should ask you about this."

Katía pulled back, eyebrows scrunched together. "About what?"

"Do you think I should get a haircut and trim my beard before the wedding?"

Katía laughed and hugged him again, hanging on. "Fitz Fitzgerald, I love you whether you have long hair and a long beard or are bald and clean-shaven … or anywhere in between. The question is, what would make you feel happiest? If you want to try a new look, do it because you want to, not because that mean-spirited man called you riffraff."

Fitz squeezed tighter, smelling her lavender-scented shampoo. "Thanks. I needed to hear that."

"I wish we could just stay here tonight."

Fitz replied, "We could if you'd just pick me up and bring me back so no one would know I'm here."

"I mean as husband and wife." She nestled into his neck.

Fitz's heart surged with temptation. His pulse quickened. His heart pounded. Somehow he found the strength to resist and said, "We agreed not till after the wedding, though."

"I know, but I can still wish."

The special moment was shattered by the sound of breaking glass. Fitz pulled Katía behind the wall, drew his Beretta, and hurried to the living room. He heard a car driving away and peeked out just in time to see taillights fading into the twilight.

Glass littered the living room floor along with a stone. Just like earlier that morning, this rock had a note attached. Fitz scowled as he read, "Too Late."

Katía hurried in behind Fitz, Glock in hand. Reading the note, she asked, "What does that mean?"

"It means something bad is coming. They might be coming back."

"Or they could just be trying to scare us," Katía said. "Either way, I guess it's good we're going to Ben's tonight."

"I think we need to get out of here. We'll have to make sure we're not followed," Fitz replied.

"I'm not leaving till I get the police out here," she said as she dialed 911.

Fitz sighed and kept watching out the broken window.

By the time the deputies finished processing the scene and Fitz and Katía had taped a piece of plastic over the broken window, it was 7:43 p.m.

"It's too late to cook," Katía said. "How about a Wendy's hamburger on the way to Ben's?"

"Meow," Buffett said.

"I'm afraid he knows what Wendy's means," Fitz said.

Katía laughed and bent down to pet Buffett. "You're too smart for your own good."

CHAPTER 21

Fitz and Katía parked along the curb at Ben's house, having driven both cars to prevent damage in case the rock thrower should return.

"I wonder what Zee's doing here," Katía said as she walked up to Fitz's car.

"That is odd." Fitz scooped up Buffett before picking up the cat carrier containing Cotton off his back seat. Katía had her bag and Snow's carrier.

"I was wonderin' if you lovebirds would ever get here," Zee teased as Fitz and Katía walked in to be greeted by sniffs from Snickers and King. Snow hissed from inside her carrier.

"We got delayed by a rock through my window," Katía said.

"What happened?" Ben asked.

"We were about to start supper when someone threw another rock. It had a note that said, 'Too late.' It took a while for the deputies to finish processing the scene, then we had to get it cleaned up and patched."

"That's scary," Ben replied.

"You're gonna have to quit talkin' to them lawyers," Zee added.

"Why's that?" Fitz asked.

"It seems like every time you talk to a lawyer, somebody throws a rock."

Fitz tugged his beard. "You're right, Zee. Unless someone is following me, I think this proves our theory that it's one of the lawyers."

"It's too many coincidences to be a coincidence," Ben said. "I think one of the lawyers is telling the thugs you're snooping around."

"If it quacks like a duck and waddles like a duck … well, you know the rest," Zee said. "It'd be nice if you just talked to one at a time. Then we'd know which one it was."

Fitz dug some M&Ms from his pocket and ate them, wondering which lawyer it could be. His heart rate sped up as he considered that one of them might be responsible for putting Katía in danger. From the whirl of his thoughts and emotions, he realized Katía was talking.

"I see the connection, but it doesn't make sense. Why would a lawyer go to this extent just because Fitz came around asking questions?"

"That's true, too," Ben said.

"It would make sense if someone were paying the lawyer to let them know if anyone is asking about the case," Fitz observed.

"But why try to scare you off?" Ben asked. "It's not like you were threatening to expose anyone."

"But I was planting the suggestion that the crime was not as it appeared," Fitz replied. "It seems whoever is behind all of this will go to great lengths to make sure it plays out the they want it to."

Ben stood up from the counter. "I hate to say this, but the next question is what are we going to do about it?"

"The note said it was too late. I expect that means they are planning to do something beyond threatening with rocks," Fitz said.

"Their favorite place seems to be the park," Zee noted. "You reckon they'll try somethin' in the mornin'?"

"Possibly. We'll have to be ready," Ben said.

"We should lay that trap we talked about yesterday," Zee said.

"That's a good idea, Zee. I can hide near the cars while the rest of you walk," Fitz said.

"It would be better if I waited with you," Ben added.

"I wonder if the rock thrower and the goons who abducted Harley and Nate are the same people," Katía suggested.

"I bet they're one and the same," Zee said. "This town's too small to have two sets of crooks like that."

Fitz finally couldn't resist asking, "So what brings you to Ben's house this time of night, Zee?"

"He invited me to the slumber party," Zee answered.

The next morning, they paraded to the park in their separate cars, pulling in right behind Luna.

"I can't believe we all got here at the same time," Luna said as everyone got out of their vehicles. "That's never happened before."

"We did all leave Ben's at the same time," Katía replied.

"Even Zee?" Luna asked.

"Yes siree," Zee answered. "You should've joined us."

Luna laughed. "Sounds like it was quite the party. Everybody ready?"

"Yeah, but Fitz and I aren't going far," Ben said. "We're going to double back in case these rock-tossers have more mischief planned."

"Are you sure that's a good idea?" Luna asked.

Fitz tugged his beard and popped some M&Ms into his mouth while Katía explained last night's incident.

"Please tell me you called the police and aren't trying to handle this on your own," Luna said.

"We did," Katía replied. "Ben and Fitz want to try catching the crooks if they come through this morning."

"Oh, Lord. Be careful. If you get shot, I'll beat you," Luna said.

Fitz laughed. "I'll make sure not to get shot then. Shall we?" He gestured toward the trail.

The group walked across the ground and onto the trail in the dull gray dawn. When they were just out of sight of the vehicles, Fitz and Ben doubled back and hid behind some large boulders near the cars.

After a moment, Ben said, "If one of us were behind the restroom building, we could come at them from two angles."

"True. I'll go," Fitz replied. He checked to see if anyone was lurking about, then hurried behind the restrooms. Leaning against the wall, he waited. *I don't think anything's going to happen. Maybe the rock at Katía's was just another threat.*

The light was still dim when Fitz heard Katía and Luna chatting as they approached. Giving up on the goons coming, Fitz took three steps to go meet the gang when car lights topped the hill, heading his way. He ducked back behind the building and yelled, "Katía, stop. Someone's coming."

As the vehicle got closer, Fitz could tell it was an SUV. Finally, it was close enough to see it was a deputy's vehicle. He came out from behind the building and called to Katía, "It's a deputy. Y'all can come on."

The car parked near the other vehicles. Two deputies got out as Fitz walked over to greet them. The other park pals arrived just as one of the deputies said, "Joe Fitzgerald?"

Fitz extended his hand. "That's me. What can I do for you?" It was a deputy Fitz didn't recognize.

"You're under arrest for the robbery of Saint Luke's United Methodist Church. Surrender your pistol."

Fitz's mouth dropped open as he handed over the gun. Katía's wide-eyed expression worried him. The rest of the park pals seemed frozen. Finally, Katía said, "That's impossible. I'm the pastor of that church and know that Fitz would never rob it. He's my fiancé. I insist that he not be arrested."

"Sorry, ma'am, but we have the warrant, and I have to execute it."

"Even if it's absurd?" Katía growled.

"Yes, ma'am."

"Even if I say the church is not pressing charges against him?"

"Yes, ma'am."

The other deputy got behind Fitz and handcuffed him.

"I need your names and badge numbers," Katía said. "I'll be sure to have you brought up for false arrest."

Luna handed Katía a pen and paper, and Katía wrote down the names and numbers. "Where are you taking him?" she demanded.

"To the county jail, ma'am."

Katía hurried over and kissed Fitz. "I'll be there before they are."

"It'll be OK," Fitz said, wishing he could reach his M&Ms.

The deputy read Fitz his Miranda rights and loaded him into the back seat. True to her word, Katía jumped into her Prius and pulled out ahead of the deputies. Fitz watched as her taillights disappeared over the hill.

CHAPTER 22

Katía's heart pounded in her chest, and her palms sweated on the steering wheel as she drove out of the park. *How dare they arrest him! I have to get him out before the wedding. This is ridiculous!* After Fitz's arrest, she had jumped into her car without even saying goodbye to the others.

She drove toward the county jail, where she had volunteered as a chaplain over the years. She thought about the little she knew of the booking process and decided she would be wasting her time going to the jail. Just as she was about to turn left to go to the expressway, she changed her mind. Turning right instead, she headed toward the sheriff's office.

Taking a deep breath to steel her nerves, she said to herself, "I'm not taking no for an answer." Katía marched into the sheriff's office and found Geraldine sitting at the desk.

"Hey, Geraldine, I need to see Sheriff Tucker. It's urgent."

"Oh? What's the problem? Maybe I can help."

Too angry to wait, Katía strode in and banged on the sheriff's door. When Sheriff Tucker opened the door, she said, "I want answers now!"

"Hello, Reverend Bancroft. It's good to see you. What might you want answers to?"

"You know what I want answers to. Why was Fitz arrested this morning for the church robbery?"

"What? You have to be kidding, … but I can see you're not. Have a seat and let me look this up."

"You mean you didn't know?"

"I have no idea what you're talking about."

"Deputies Lassiter and Kindall showed up at Laurel Park this morning and arrested Fitz. I consider that a brazen misuse of power."

Sheriff Tucker sat down at his desk and worked the computer. His eyes narrowed as he studied the screen. Katía sat stiffly in her chair, trying to hold her tongue.

After a couple of minutes, Sheriff Tucker said, "I see that Warren Windsor of the DA's office issued the arrest warrant. For probable cause, it says Fitz would have known about the offering money and would be in need of funds since he is homeless."

"That's the most absurd thing I've ever heard! There is absolutely no evidence and the probable cause is just made up!"

Sheriff Tucker held up his hands. "Calm down, Reverend Bancroft. I'm on your side. I see what you're saying and can't imagine why Windsor thought his suspicions warranted an arrest. I'll talk to him and find out what's going on."

Sheriff Tucker stood, but Katía remained seated. "I'm not leaving till we get this resolved."

With a sigh, Sheriff Tucker sat down and called the district attorney's office. "Warren Windsor, please. This is Sheriff Tucker."

Katía noticed he avoided eye contact with her while he waited for Windsor to pick up.

"Hi, Mr. Windsor, Sheriff Tucker here. I need to know what basis you have for arresting Joe Fitzgerald. We're already being threatened with a lawsuit for false arrest. … I see. That sounds like nothing more than conjecture, and you know it won't hold up in court. … I assume you're feeling pressure to make an arrest in this case, but I really don't want to try defending a lawsuit based on what you've told me. I think we need to let the man go. … So you're going to force me to talk to your boss, then? Will you transfer me, or do I need to call back? … That's more like it. I expect him to be released before lunchtime."

Katía was still shaking but felt the tension scaling down. She took a deep breath and exhaled slowly. The words, "released before lunchtime," anchored her heart enough that it quit pounding her ribs. She leaned back as hope blossomed.

Sheriff Tucker hung up the phone and said, "You were right. They had no case. With the threat of his boss finding out, Mr. Windsor saw the light."

"I can't thank you enough!" Katía beamed.

"I bet Fitz will be relieved to see you. If you want to drive on over to the jail, I'll call and make sure the process of releasing him is started." He stood from his desk and held out his hand.

Katía rounded the desk and hugged him. "Thanks again!" she said as she hurried out of the office.

"What in the world was that about?" Geraldine asked as Katía passed by her desk.

"They arrested Fitz for robbing my church. I needed help getting him released."

"I know Fitz can stir up trouble, but he ain't no thief," Geraldine said.

"I hope you'll be able to make it to our wedding Saturday."

"If you can keep Fitz out of jail, I'll be there," Geraldine replied.

Katía tried to stay reasonably close to the speed limit as she drove to the jail. When she got there, she reported to the woman at the front desk that she was there to pick up Joe Fitzgerald.

The woman scowled at her and while typing his name into the computer and said, "Ma'am, they are just in the process of booking him. He's not going to be released anytime soon."

Her scowl turned into confusion as she studied her screen. "What in the world? Can't say as I've ever seen this before. There's an order to let him go. It looks like they're in the process of returning his clothes. He should be ready to go soon. You can have a seat."

"Thank you very much." Katía sat down and gasped. *I'd better let the others know what's happening.* She pulled up the park pals' group text and explained what she had done and that she was now waiting for Fitz to be released. Expressions of congratulations and relief popped up instantly from Ben, Luna, and Zee.

While she waited, Katía closed her eyes and prayed. *I am grateful, Lord, that Fitz is getting out of jail. Thank you for using Sheriff Tucker as an instrument of justice. Amen.*

When she opened her eyes, Fitz was standing in front of her. Katía leapt into his arms, tears welling in her eyes. While Fitz held her tightly, she said, "You'd better not ever do that to me again."

Fitz laughed. "It wasn't exactly my fault. I suppose you're behind my getting released, for which I'm extremely grateful."

Katía explained her trip to see Sheriff Tucker while she drove to the park to pick up Fitz's car. When they arrived at Ben's house, they were greeted with a banner that Ben had printed off: WELCOME BACK JAILBIRD!

Ben, Zee, and Luna had also prepared a spread for lunch but insisted Katía explain what had happened first. After she related the story, Zee said, "At least we know which lawyer's behind these threats now, but that was a rough way to find out."

"I hope we've learned our lesson," Luna said. "I think it's time to let this go … let the police do their job for once."

The group went silent, then Luna said, "That's not going to happen, is it?"

CHAPTER 23

At Ben's house, while everyone was digging into their sandwiches, Katía noticed Fitz was staring into space. "What are you so deep in thought about? I hope it's me," she said with a grin.

"I'm wondering what the connection is between this lawyer and Harley and Nate. Why would Windsor be worried about their cases so much that he would send rock-throwing maniacs after us and risk his career by orchestrating my arrest?" Fitz answered.

"I was afraid you weren't thinking about me," Katía said, feigning sadness.

Fitz tugged his beard. "I think about you most of the time."

"I was teasing, Fitz. Obviously, Windsor either has something to gain or something to lose from these cases."

"Yeah, but what?" Fitz asked.

"Money or death," Zee said.

"How do you figure that?" Fitz asked.

"I reckon there's two ways he stands to gain. Either he's looking to advance his career by two court victories, or somebody's paying him to inform them if anything could risk the cases goin' off-rail."

"What about the death part?" Luna asked.

"That's easy. If he doesn't cooperate, somebody's threatenin' to kill 'im," Zee replied.

"You sure know how to think like a criminal. It's kind of spooky," Ben said.

"It's a gift," Zee grinned.

"Unless he's just totally looney, I don't think he'd have me arrested just to stop me from looking into Harley and Nate's cases. I'm betting there's somebody either bribing or threatening him," Fitz said.

"Or both," Katía added. "We need to find out who and why."

"But how?" Luna asked.

"That's the million-dollar question," Zee said, taking a bite of his sandwich.

"We could just go ask him," Ben said, mischief playing at his eyes.

"I'm sure he'd be glad to tell us," Luna snarked.

"No, but if we poke the bear, he might attack," Ben replied.

"That's the last thing we need," Luna said. "We're trying to make it to a wedding this Saturday, remember?"

"If we're ready for the attack, we could put an end to all of this," Ben added.

"How can we set a trap when we don't know if, when, or how the attack will be coming?" Luna pointed out.

"So far their targets have been the park and Katía's house. Since nobody's going to be at Katía's, that leaves the park. I know the deputies showed up this morning, but I bet somebody else will show up tomorrow. Fitz and I can question the good attorney this afternoon."

"No, it can't be you," Katía observed.

"Why not?" Ben asked.

"Because your house is our safe space. We can't let him know you're involved. We need to keep Luna and Zee out of it, too. It'll have to be Fitz and me," Katía said.

"That narrows it down to me," Fitz said.

"Why just you?" Katía asked.

"Because they've already threatened you. I don't want to give them any more reason to come after you."

Katía's hands went to her hips. "Well, they've already arrested you. So far, I have the better record. If anyone goes alone, it should be me."

Fitz took a bite of the sandwich to give himself time to think. He needed an argument against what she was saying, but none volunteered. Finally, he spoke from his heart. "Please don't. Just let me go. I'll feel better knowing you're not in danger."

"They know we're a couple, Fitz. Whether or not I go with you, I'm still at risk. Remember the rock through my window? I might be able to help drag some information out of him."

Fitz sighed.

"She's got a point," Zee said. "She could tell him she's there to hear his confession."

Fitz glared at Zee. "OK, I give. We'll go together," Fitz replied.

Fitz and Katía timed their arrival at Windsor's office for two o'clock, in case he was out for a long lunch. Fitz held the door as Katía walked into the office and watched as she walked up to the severe-looking secretary's desk.

"Hi, Ms. Underwood, I'm Reverend Bancroft. We need to speak with Mr. Windsor."

Fitz was amazed to see the scowl on her face soften as she replied, "I'll see if he's available." Just as she stood, the interior door opened, and Windsor stepped out, file in hand.

The surprise on his face contorted into a grimace. "Audrey, this is ready to be filed."

"Of course. This is Reverend Bancroft. She was asking if she could speak with you."

"I'm busy." He turned toward his office.

"It will just take a second, sir," Katía said.

"I assume you're here because you're mad about Fitz's arrest. I've noted your concerns. Now I need to get back to work."

"I'll be happy to ask my questions in front of Ms. Underwood," Katía said, a threatening tone in her voice. When Windsor hesitated, she said, "For example, each time Fitz has talked with you…"

Windsor cut her off. "Come in."

Fitz followed Windsor and Katía into his office, amazed at how she had gotten them in. *It looks like I should let her do the talking.*

"What exactly are you getting at?" Windsor growled.

Katía's spine stiffened. "Each time Fitz has had contact with you, a rock has been thrown through one of our windows. I don't think it's a coincidence."

"I have no idea what you're talking about," Windsor said.

"Here's something you do have an idea about. Why did you have Fitz arrested?" Katía pushed.

"Because I believe he is the most likely suspect. I still think so," he said, glaring at Fitz.

"I believe it is because someone is paying you to scare him away from Harley and Nate's cases. Who's paying you, Mr. Windsor?"

Fitz noted Windsor's hesitation and knew Katía had rattled him.

Windsor walked behind his desk. "That's absurd. Are you going to leave, or do I need to call security?"

"We're going, but I hope you realize your career will go down the drain when you go to prison for this."

Fitz followed Katía out. When they were in the elevator, he said, "You were amazing! You definitely poked the bear." Taking her hand, he could tell she was shaking. "You OK?"

"I'm not sure if I'm more nervous or more angry. It's definitely a mixture of both."

"I'm glad you came along. I wouldn't have gotten that far with him."

"I just hope he doesn't do something really bad."

CHAPTER 24

The park pals arrived at Laurel Park at their usual time on Thursday morning and set out on their walk without the dogs and Buffett, having left them at Ben's house. Just like yesterday morning, Fitz and Ben doubled back, Ben taking up a position behind the large rocks and Fitz behind the bathhouse.

Once Katía, Luna, and Zee were out of sight of the cars on the other side of the park, they cut through the woods and hid behind a set of bleachers at the ball field.

Fitz saw their shadowy forms as the three of them took up their positions. *I hope they keep still so they're not noticed.* Keeping an eye out for an incoming vehicle, he called Katía. "If someone comes, stay down and keep still. I can see you from here."

"Yes, sir," Katía answered. "That was our plan, anyway." As Fitz watched, they crouched down and disappeared.

"How's that?" Katía asked.

"Perfect."

Settling in to wait, Fitz leaned against the wall. A memory that had not surfaced in years tracked across his mind. It was more a feeling than a thought.

Four days after he had walked out of his house with the intention of living in his car, he was watching the sunset. A feeling of euphoria came over him as he realized all the bills he would no longer be tied to. No more rent. No cable bill. No electric bill. *I felt so free, but I soon learned I was still chained to myself and the alcohol. I wonder how much I spent on alcohol before Buffett rescued me that day at Popeyes.*

He smiled. *I wish I had a picture of Buffett and me then. We both looked grungy the day I met him.*

With a sigh, his thoughts moved to his current appearance. *I wish Katía had given me a straight answer about the hair and beard.* Another smile. *I'll be back to paying all those bills soon. It'll be worth it since I'll have Katía to share life with.*

The sound of his phone pinging dragged him from his thoughts. Opening the text app, he realized he had missed a previous text because he was zoned out. They were both from Katía, asking how much longer he thought they should wait.

Checking his watch, he realized he had been swimming around in his thoughts for thirty minutes. He texted back, "If they haven't come by now, I don't think they will. They seem to be good at timing it while we're away from the cars."

"Unless they're timing it to be sure we're back," Katía texted back.

It was a chilling thought, but Fitz's gut still told him they weren't going to show. He walked to the front of the bathhouse and waved.

Ben was the first to arrive. "Well, that was a waste of time."

"Yep," Fitz replied.

Walking up, Luna said, "I hope the arrest was all they meant by 'Too late' on the note."

"Maybe so, but I can't believe they would give up that easily," Fitz replied.

Katía sidled up to Fitz and put her arm around him. "See you for lunch?"

"Of course," Fitz replied. "Your house, or do you want to eat out?"

"Let's say our house. I need to get to the office. It's my last day of work before the wedding!" She gave him a kiss and headed for her Prius.

After the park pals left, Fitz decided he wanted to surprise Katía with a gift. It was still too early for the store he wanted to shop at to open, so he went to the library to read the paper. It was the usual fare of subdivisions starting, restaurants opening or closing, and who had been in court for what crime. He also turned in his library book and searched the stacks till he picked out his next one.

After stowing the book in his car, Fitz walked to Rahab's Rope on the square. He found a necklace strung with tiny animals and a cross, all of which were carved out of walnut.

She'll love this! The clerk gift-wrapped it, and Fitz drove to Katía's house.

It was 11:00 a.m. when he arrived, so he made himself useful by cleaning the bathrooms and running the vacuum. He was ready and waiting at 12:00 p.m.

He placed the gift on the kitchen table and sat sipping iced tea while he waited for her to get there. Snow, Cotton, and Buffett set up a chorus of meows, so Fitz dished out some treats for them. That seemed to satisfy them, and they returned to the den.

Fitz checked his watch: 12:26 p.m. *I wonder what's taking her so long.* Before he knew it, he was pacing from the kitchen to the den and back. At 12:43, he called, but she didn't answer. *Something's wrong.* He hurried out the door and drove to the church.

Seeing her car parked in its usual spot brought a sense of relief. *Maybe she was just on the phone and couldn't pick up.* He grabbed his Beretta anyway. Walking into her office, he found her laptop open and a cup of cold coffee on the desk, but no Katía.

Panic surged. "Katía! Katía!" He ran to the bathroom door and called there before hurrying into the sanctuary. Fear and rage collided with the realization that she wasn't there. He hurried through the Sunday school wing and fellowship hall just to be sure, but his mind had already jumped to the worst-case scenario. *This is what that rock meant!*

Pulling his beard and eating M&Ms, Fitz tried to make sense of what was going on and to figure out what to do. The shock was squeezing his heart, and he felt dizzy. He sat down in one of the chairs in her office.

"I have to pull myself together," he said to the void. After one more round of M&Ms, he took slow, deep breaths and called Ben.

"Hey, Fitz, what's up?"

"I don't know what to do."

"What do you mean? What's wrong?"

"Katía's gone! I think they took her!"

"Are you sure?"

"I'm at the church. Her car's here, but she's not. What should I do?"

"Have you called the police?"

Embarrassment mixed with fear and anger, roiling in Fitz's heart. "Not yet. I should have done that first."

"You call 911. I'm on my way."

After Fitz placed the call and reported Katía's abduction, he remained seated in the chair, unable to bring himself to leave her office. He thought of all the times he had visited her in this room, the chats and laughter they had shared. Now she was gone. Just like Sharon. Gone. No warning. Just gone.

Sweat mingled with rapid breathing and a racing heart. He tried to push away the memory of the call that had reported Sharon's death, but it refused to leave.

"Katía's not dead! She's not dead! She can't be dead! Oh, God, please bring her back to me!"

A hand touched his shoulder, and he jumped. Looking up, he saw Ben standing over him. Looking down, he realized he was lying on the floor.

"Fitz, we're going to get her back," Ben said.

"I left Buffett at the house."

"I'm sure Buffett will be fine."

"But I need him. He's the one who always gets me through these episodes."

"I know I'm not as furry as Buffett, but right now you're stuck with me," Ben replied. "Did you call 911?"

Fitz nodded.

"OK, then. Would it be a good idea to get up and sit in the chair?"

Fitz nodded again and pushed himself off the floor. Ben pulled a tissue from the box on Katía's desk and handed it to him.

Wiping his face, Fitz said, "I sort of lost it."

"I don't blame you. This is quite a shock. I trust you searched the church."

Another nod. Fitz's spine stiffened at the sound of a car pulling up. Ben hurried to the door.

"It's a couple of deputies," Ben reported.

Fitz stood, then sat back down as a wave of dizziness washed over him. Deputy James entered, trailed by a medium-height, muscular man.

"Hey, Fitz. Ben," Diann James said. "This is Nolan Henderson, one of our newest deputies. Tell me what happened."

"Do you know about the rock thrown through Katía's window?" Fitz asked.

"Yeah, I read the report."

"She was supposed to meet me at her house for lunch. When she didn't show up, I came here and found…" Having difficulty saying the words, Fitz waved his arm around the room as if that would explain.

"He found her car here, but she's missing," Ben explained.

"Nolan, would you request an APB to be put out for Katía Bancroft?"

"Sure, but I'll need a photo and other demographics."

"Either of you have a photo?" Diann asked.

Fitz pulled out his phone. Wishing his hand would quit shaking, he located a photo of her he had taken while they were having lunch on the square. He showed it to Diann.

"Perfect. Text it to Nolan. What's your number, Nolan?"

While Fitz was entering Nolan's number to text the photo, the church door opened and footsteps sounded in the hall. Zee's head popped into the doorway.

"I can't believe this is happenin'. Hey, deputies. Did you tell 'em about that lawyer yet?"

"Zee doesn't beat around the bush," Ben said.

"Get that APB going, Nolan." Turning to Fitz, Diann asked, "What about this lawyer?"

Fitz sighed. "We believe the prosecuting attorney for the two recent burglary cases involving residentially-challenged people is behind the threats we've been receiving. Katía and I went to talk to him again yesterday, and today she's gone."

"Who's the attorney?" Diann asked.

"Warren Windsor," Ben answered.

"Do you have any proof?" Diann asked.

"He's battin' four for three," Zee said. "Fitz talked to him three times and got one note, two rocks, then this."

Diann took photos, and she and Nolan searched every room of the church to be sure Fitz had not missed anything.

Just before she left, she asked, "Do you really think Windsor is behind this?"

Fitz nodded. "My gut tells me he is."

"Hmm. Obviously, this doesn't give me cause to arrest him, but I'll certainly keep his name in mind as we proceed."

Fitz offered Diann his hand. "You have to find her."

"We'll do our best. Call me if you think of anything else," she said, handing him her card.

With the deputies gone, Fitz plopped back into the same chair he had been sitting in earlier. Hanging his head in his hands, he said, "Why didn't I stop when I had the chance?"

"Because innocent folks' lives are at stake, and quittin' ain't what we do," Zee answered. "You've got to pull yourself together so we can find Katía."

CHAPTER 25

Fitz ate a few M&Ms, looked around the church office, then started to close Katía's computer.

"Wait, we might need that," Ben said.

Fitz eyed him, scrunching his eyebrows together.

"It probably requires a password to open it," Ben explained.

Zee said, "I wonder if any of the folks across the street saw anything."

"Zee, you're brilliant," Fitz said, a crack of hope opening in his heart. "There's a neighbor who's always keeping an eye on what's going on around here. Let's pay her a visit." He hurried out the door with Zee and Ben in tow. Crossing the street, he headed straight for Irma Mae's porch.

When she opened the door, she said, "My! Three gentlemen callers at the same time."

Fitz cut to the chase. "Katía's been abducted. Did you see any cars coming and going today?"

"Oh, my! Come in. I did see a car pull up around nine-thirty. It was red. I didn't think much of it at the time, ... silly me, have a seat." The three men remained standing. "Anyway, as I was saying, I didn't think much of it at the time because people come and go at the church. When I heard it crank up, I naturally looked out the window again. This time, it seemed odd that Katía was in the car with them."

"You saw her in the car?" Fitz gasped.

"Yeah. I don't know what possessed me, even though I thought she was probably just going to a meeting, but the two guys looked kind of mean, so I took a picture. I probably shouldn't have, but I did."

"Irma Mae, I need that picture," Fitz said louder than he had meant to.

"Well, yes, of course." She pulled her phone out of her pocket. "My daughter texts me pictures, but I don't know how to do that."

"Do you mind if I help?" Ben asked. "I'm Ben Blessing, by the way, and this is Zee Jameson. We're friends of Fitz and Katía. Thank you," he said as she handed him her phone. He texted it using the park pals' group text. Fitz and Zee's phones pinged.

"I hope she's going to be OK. Let me know if I can help," Irma Mae called as the three men hurried out her door.

"You already have," Ben called.

Fitz stopped in the middle of the road. "I have to text this to Diann."

"You might want to get out of the road before you do," Zee pointed out.

Moving to the shoulder, Fitz entered Diann's number and sent her the text with an explanation. *I'm grateful Katia showed me how to do this.* Studying the car, he realized the tag was in the photo.

"Hey, Ben, is there a way to enlarge the photo?"

"I already have. The tag's too blurry to make out. I might be able to find a program that can enhance it."

While Fitz's heart crashed, his phone pinged with a text from Diann. "That's wonderful. I'll get it to the lab. I hope they can enhance the photo enough to read the tag number."

"At least we know they're driving a red Camaro." Zee said. "Why do bad people always seem to have nice cars?"

Fitz texted Diann back. "Thanks. Please let me know if they find out who the car belongs to."

Diann's response came back quickly. "We'll see. I'm not sure that's such a good idea."

Fitz glared at his phone but resisted responding in anger. Shutting off the screen, he headed for the church. "I guess we need to lock up," he said, heart wrenching. He wanted to get in his car and search for her but had no idea where to look.

"Should we drive her car to the house? We can come back and get the one we leave here." Ben asked.

"I'm sure the keys are in her purse," Fitz said. "I don't remember seeing it in the church."

Head down, he went into the church and looked around her office. The purse wasn't there. He turned off the light while Ben unplugged the computer without shutting it down.

"I'm taking this with us just in case. Does she usually lock her office door?"

Fitz tugged his beard. "I don't know. I wonder if we should let someone in the church know what's happened."

"Who would we call?" Zee asked.

"There's a lady named Hope ... Hope McKinley. She's the head of some committee. Shirley's going to be in the wedding, but I can't remember her last name," Fitz replied.

Setting the computer on the desk, Ben sat down and hunted through her files till he found one named "Members." He opened it up, scrolled down to the Ms, and found Hope. "You ready?" he asked.

Fitz stared at his phone, not answering.

"OK, I'll call," Ben said.

When Ben disconnected after informing Hope of Katía's abduction, Zee said, "You're gonna say I'm brilliant, but I just figured out who might could get that tag number."

"Who's that?" Fitz asked.

"Ole Cullin Patton. He's an artist who does most of his art on the computer."

"How would that help?" Fitz asked, not following.

"He would have the type of program that can enhance the image," Ben explained. "Zee, you are brilliant. Let's call him."

"I don't know his number, but I know where his studio is," Zee explained.

Fitz hurried toward the door. "Well, come on!" He rushed out the door and into Ben's car.

Ben parked near the old First Methodist Church, the parsonage of which had been turned into a studio for artists. Ben asked, "If he does his art on the computer, why does he need a studio?"

"He does some paintin', too," Zee said. "Mostly I think he likes to be around the other artists. He's all by himself in this ole world."

Zee banged on the door, and a lady cracked it open. "Oh, hey, Zee." She opened it wider. "What are you up to?"

"I'm hopin' Cullin's here."

"He sure is. Come on in." She started to close the door behind Zee.

"They're with me," Zee explained.

They made their way upstairs to a small room where a man with a long brown ponytail sat at a computer. A dozen paintings sat on the floor along the wall, and several were hung haphazardly around the room.

"Well, look what the cat drug in! Hey, Zee," Cullin said, standing to shake his hand.

"Hey, Cullin. This is Fitz and Ben. We need a favor."

"Um hmm. What might that be?" Cullin asked, eyes narrowing just a bit.

"You see, a friend of ours, actually she's Fitz's fiancé, has been abducted."

"That's terrible," Cullin said.

"We have a blurry photo of the car and wondered if you would mind tryin' to enhance the image so we could read the tag number," Zee continued.

"Sure, I can try," Cullin said, sitting back down. "Where's the photo?"

Fitz emailed it to Cullin. "Let's see what kind of magic we can work." Working the mouse, he added, "This might take a minute."

Fitz popped M&Ms into his mouth and studied the paintings. One in particular tugged at his heart, though he couldn't figure out why at first. It was an abstract work. The more Fitz studied it, the more he felt he was seeing a moon shining on a creek in the woods. Though he wasn't sure what the painting was supposed to be, it spoke to him. "You're still with me. I can't lose Katía like I did you. I just can't."

"What was that?" Ben asked.

Fitz tugged his beard. "Nothing. Just talking to myself."

"Would you look at that," Cullin said. "I can make out all but one of the characters on the tag."

Fitz flew to look over Cullin's shoulder. "We have to write that down!"

Cullin wrote the tag number onto a notepad. "Wait, let me try one more thing." After a couple of clicks of the mouse, the last character appeared to be a B or an 8. Fitz jotted down the number, ending it with B/8.

"Thank you so much. We have to go," Fitz said, hurrying out the door.

Ben followed, and Zee stopped long enough to say, "Thanks so much. We need to get together for lunch again sometime." He hurried to catch up.

CHAPTER 26

As soon as Fitz stepped out the studio door, he called the sheriff's office and asked for Geraldine.

"Hi, Geraldine, it's Fitz. I need you to run two license plate numbers."

"Oh, no. Now what are you into? This doesn't have anything to do with Katía does it?"

"Of course not. I'm looking at buying a car and want to make sure the seller is who he says he is." He noticed Zee's grin, then gave Geraldine the tag numbers. "I can't remember if the last number is an eight or a B."

He heard the clicking of the keyboard as Geraldine said, "The first one is a Ford Escape belonging to Virginia Watson, and the second is a Camaro belonging to Eddie Marsh."

"Marsh is the one. You got an address for him?"

Geraldine hesitated. "If you went to see the car, don't you know where he lives?"

"Um, we met at Walmart," Fitz cringed. He caught Zee suppressing a laugh.

"I can't believe you'd buy a Camaro right before your wedding. OK, here's the address."

Fitz wrote down the address and thanked Geraldine before disconnecting the call. "Let's go."

"Don't you think you should give the sheriff's department that information?" Ben asked.

"I'll call Diann on the way. Come on." Fitz headed toward Ben's car.

When Zee caught up, he laughed. "That was a doozy! Where'd you learn to fib on the fly like that?"

"I didn't think she'd give me the info if she knew the real reason I wanted it. It was a tactical lie," Fitz replied.

In the car, Fitz texted Diann the photo of the car, the driver's name, the address, and the tag number. "This is who abducted Katía," he concluded.

Diann texted back, "Impressive. We should get you on the force. Now leave it alone!"

"What did she say?" Ben asked.

"She commended me on my detective work," Fitz answered.

"And?" Ben replied.

"She said to leave it alone."

"I see. Well, it can't hurt to pay this guy a friendly visit," Ben said.

The GPS app led them out Skelton Road, past the Lowe's, and to a street on the right. Ben confirmed the location by the number on the mailbox.

"I don't see that Camaro," Zee observed.

"Muttering magpies, the lock-picking kit is in my car," Fitz said. "Let's at least knock."

Fitz wasn't surprised when no one answered. After testing the knob and finding it locked, he said "Let's check the windows."

Ben went to the right, while Fitz and Zee went left. The second window was too high for Fitz to see into, but Zee was tall enough.

"This is one of the perks of tallness," Zee chuckled. "It's kind of hard to see through the sheers, but I don't believe she's in there."

When they met around back, Ben said, "I didn't see anything. We could let the dogs out and see if they seem to recognize her scent."

"I don't think they brought her here at all. She's being held somewhere else," Fitz said.

"You're most likely right," Ben replied. "Well, now what?"

"Has anybody eaten lunch? I'm starvin'," Zee said.

"Why don't we stop at the Wendy's down the road and figure out our next move?" Ben suggested.

Fitz walked back to the car without a word, head down.

At Wendy's, Fitz sat down with his lunch, dragged a French fry through the ketchup, and stopped with it in midair. The fry seemed so heavy, and he felt so drained.

"Hang in there. We're gonna find 'er," Zee said.

"I'm not sure I can go on if we don't," Fitz mumbled.

"Well, don't let that happen, then," Zee replied. "We gotta get the fight back in you."

"That's right," Ben agreed, sitting down. "Our next move is to figure out all we can about this guy so we can discern where he might hide a hostage."

Ben pulled out his phone and dialed Luna. "I'm going to get her to hunt him down on social media."

Fitz found the strength to eat that French fry after Ben and Zee's encouragement.

"Maybe they took 'er to that other guy's house, the one in the back seat with 'er," Zee suggested.

"That's possible. I wouldn't want to hold a hostage in my house, though," Ben replied after explaining the situation to Luna.

"I bet whoever is orchestrating all of this has a property where they're holding her. We need to figure out who that is," Fitz said.

A tray fell across the restaurant, eliciting such a jump from Fitz that he would have knocked over the table had it not been bolted to the floor. Instead, the table sent him crashing back into his seat.

"I think you're stressed," Ben observed.

"You think? I have to get Katía back." He pushed a fry around.

"Let's eat while we wait to see what Luna digs up," Ben suggested.

Silence pressed down on Fitz as he took tentative bites, his mind grinding to find a way forward. It dawned on him his emotions were preventing him from thinking clearly. *This is what it means when they tell an officer they're too close to the case. I have to get control of myself.* He took a deep breath and let it out slowly. It didn't help. He checked his watch: 2:14 p.m. Ben's phone rang, prompting another jump.

He listened as Ben talked to Luna and watched as he scribbled notes on a napkin. Fitz startled again when his phone rang. "It's Katía!" Answering, he said, "Hey, are you OK?"

A man's voice spoke. "My cameras told me you and some friends were snooping around my house. You just brought your bride one step closer to death." The man disconnected, and the world faded. Fitz's heart pounded with panic.

"That wasn't Katía," Zee noted.

It took a minute, but Fitz finally managed to speak. "They saw us on camera at his house. He said we brought her one step closer to death."

"That's not going to happen on our watch," Ben said. "Luna thinks she might have found the other guy. There's one man he interacts a lot with named Carl Aikins."

"Let's get his address and pay him a visit," Fitz growled.

"Nobody'll be there," Zee said.

"Why would you say that?" Ben asked.

"Because he's with the other guy wherever they're holding Katía or at work so nobody will suspect he was involved," Zee replied.

"At least we can see where he lives," Fitz said.

"Yeah, but that'll put us on their radar again. You don't want to give 'em another reason to follow through on their threat, do you?" Zee explained.

Fitz slammed his fist onto the table, prompting the other customers to stare. The rage and frustration broke out as sweat in his palms. "I have to do something! Where could they be holding her?"

As if in answer to his question, his phone rang. "It's them again," he said after seeing Katía's name on the caller ID.

"What do you want this time?" he growled as he answered the phone.

"It's nice to talk to you, too," Katía replied.

"Katía? I was expecting the creeps who kidnapped you," Fitz said, noting that she sounded out of breath. "Are you OK?"

"Yeah. I got away. I need you to pick me up."

"Where are you, and I'll be there as soon as I can."

"I'm running down Dorsey Street. Heading kind of south toward the airport, I think. Get here. I have to keep running." She disconnected the call.

Eyes wide and pulse pounding, hope replacing the rage, Fitz said, "Come on! She got away, and we have to pick her up. I think they're after her." He got up so fast, he hit the table, and it knocked him back into his seat again. His second attempt successful, he rushed out the door. Zee caught up as Fitz and Ben settled into their seats.

"She said she's running south on Dorsey Street," Fitz explained.

"My old neck of the woods," Ben said since he used to work in that area. He gunned the Outback and raced out of the parking lot. "I'm going to start on the north end and drive south.

As he drove down Dorsey St., nearing its intersection with Industrial Blvd., Fitz pointed. "That's her!"

Ben beeped the horn and screeched to a stop beside her. Fitz pushed open the door, and she jumped into the car. As soon as she was in, Ben took off again.

Fitz wrapped her in his arms. His heart ached as he took in the fear in her eyes.

"How'd you get away from those creeps?" Zee asked.

Still out of breath, Katía explained, "They never thought to check my purse. I guess they didn't think a pastor would have a gun. I told them I had to pee, so they untied me from the chair. When I came out of the bathroom, I had my gun drawn and told them not to move. Both of their pistols were on the table. One of 'em reached for his gun, and I think I shot off a finger. I grabbed both of their pistols and my phone and ran."

"It's good to have you back," Fitz said.

Ben pulled into a gas station on Industrial Blvd. "Did you call the police?"

"No. I guess I should have held them at gunpoint and called, but I was too scared."

"I don't blame you," Zee said. "I'd've skedaddled just as fast as I could."

Ben dialed 911 and explained the situation. "I don't suppose you know the address of the building," he asked Katía.

"No, but I'm sure I'll recognize it when I see it."

Ben relayed that information, then disconnected the call. "They said for us to stay here. They're sending an officer, and we'll try to find the building."

"I'm sure the goons are long gone by now," Zee said.

"Probably," Katía replied. "But I did tell them I'd be standing outside the door waiting for the police."

Zee laughed. "That was brilliant. They might still be just sittin' there."

CHAPTER 27

Three patrol cars, lights strobing and sirens blazing, converged on the gas station where Fitz, Katía, Ben, and Zee waited.

"That oughta get some attention," Zee said.

Ben led the way and, per the officer's instructions, parked just past the building Katía identified. She pointed it out to one of the officers.

"Stay in the car until we clear the building," the officer, whose name was Gary, ordered.

"This place is a dump," Zee observed while they waited. "They could've at least taken you to a nicer place."

The building was an abandoned, dilapidated place that might have been a marine repair shop at one time. There was a single door on the street side. Ben, Fitz, Zee, and Katía twisted and looked out the back window, watching as the officers prepared to enter the building.

After two officers went around the back, Katía said, "I should have told them I have their guns."

"They'd still enter like the men were armed," Fitz said. "It's the only safe thing to do."

One officer jerked the front door open, and the one named Gary yelled, "Gainesville City Police," as he entered. The second one came right behind.

It took less than two minutes for Gary to come back. "The building's empty. We need you to give us as many details as possible."

The four of them got out of the car, and Katía said, "I have their guns."

Gary raised his eyebrows. "Impressive." He donned nylon gloves. "I'll need those for evidence." Katía handed them over, and Gary bagged and tagged them.

Inside the building, Katía explained how the men had come into the church, both aiming handguns at her. "They zip-tied my wrists and forced me into their car, which was a red Camaro. When they got me here, they tied me to the chair."

"Do you have any idea why they abducted you?" Gary asked.

"It's because of the two unhoused men who were arrested for robberies after being found unconscious at the scenes. We've been looking into those cases, and someone doesn't like that," Katía stated.

"We have the abductors' names and the Camaro's tag number," Fitz added.

Gary's eyebrows scrunched together. "Are you going to take me to them, too?"

Fitz noted the sarcasm but didn't let it get to him. He told Gary the names, addresses, and tag number of the car they had identified.

"You've been busy," Katía said.

"You didn't think we could sit back and relax while they had you, did you?" Ben asked.

"No. I'm sorry I caused so much worry."

Fitz pulled her into a hug. "You're worth worrying about."

Katía pulled back. "Oh, Gary, I shot one of the guys in the hand. I think I hit a finger, so he might head to the ER."

"Thanks. We'll put out an alert." Having already pulled up photos of the two men Fitz had identified, Gary asked, "Do these two look like the men who abducted you?"

"That's them." She pointed to Eddie Marsh. "That's the one I shot. He was reaching for his gun after I told him not to."

"Well, all right then. Y'all've given us a tremendous start on catching these guys. If you're interested, the police force is hiring."

Once they were through at the scene and back in Ben's car, Katía said, "That was an ordeal. I need ice cream." Laying her hand down on the seat, she noticed a hard, smooth surface. "Wait, is that my computer?"

"Yep. We thought we might need it," Ben explained. Not needing to ask where Katía wanted to go for ice cream, Ben drove to the nearest Dairy Queen.

"I'm starving, but I'm having a sundae first before real food."

"I'd say you've earned that," Zee said.

The park pals settled at a table with their ice creams. "I'd better let Luna know you're safe," Ben said and sent her a text.

"If you were those guys, what would you do now, Fitz?" Katía asked.

"Oh, no," Zee said. "Don't you think you've had enough excitement for one day?"

Katía held her sundae spoon in the air for emphasis. "There's still something bad going on. Even if the police catch my abductors, it's just the tip of the iceberg. What if the police don't pursue it beyond catching those two guys? They're just the small fish."

"Did they say who the big fish was?" Zee asked.

"No. I asked, though. Now, what do you think their next step will be?"

Fitz popped some M&Ms into his mouth. "I think it's a question of what will the one in charge do next rather than what the abductors will do. I imagine the boss will consider the abductors compromised and abandon them. If the boss is smart, the two guys who grabbed you don't even know their name. I imagine the big fish will find some other low-lifes to do their dirty work."

"That means you and Katía are still not safe," Ben pointed out. "Now that we know the extent to which they're willing to go, we need to take even more precautions."

Fitz sighed. He was tired of hiding, of being cautious, but Katía's safety was the most important thing to him. "You got any suggestions?"

"Yeah. You bring your gun into the house at night. If Zee stays, that'll give us more firepower if anyone shows up."

"Me and King would be happy to help."

Luna flew across the restaurant and came in fast for a hug, nearly knocking Katía out of her chair. "Oh, my God! You're safe! I'm so happy! How'd you get away?"

Katía regained her balance as Ben said, "I might have let her know we were here."

Katía relayed the story of her escape to Luna.

"They didn't catch the bad guys?" Luna said. "That's not good. They'll really be after you now."

"Fitz thinks whoever hired them will fire them, and they won't be a threat anymore."

"I didn't say that," Fitz said. "The part about firing them is likely, but you can still identify them. If they don't silence you, their chance of going to prison is much greater."

"Well, that's scary," Zee said, looking at his ice cream like it had soured.

Katía jabbed her spoon toward Fitz. "You sure know how to ruin a celebration."

Fitz shrugged his shoulders, took a bite of his Blizzard, and said, "I can't help it if I'm practical."

Katía reached across the table, and Fitz took her hand. "I love you anyway," she said.

"At least Ben's house is still a safe place.." Luna asked.

"Uh-oh! Not anymore," Zee said, pointing to the red Camaro turning into the parking lot.

CHAPTER 28

itz motioned for everyone to duck.

"I don't suppose they just happened to fancy an ice cream," Ben said.

"Nope. They followed us," Fitz replied. He eyed Luna, who already had her phone out to dial 911.

"What? If you think I'm not calling the police, you're nuts."

"Definitely call but do it from the other side of the restaurant so they won't think you're with us. When we get out of here, we'll meet at your house. Stay here till those goats leave."

"Good idea," Luna replied, then casually sauntered over to the other side of the room as she continued her call.

"She should be an actress," Zee said.

"We need to get out of here," Ben added.

"Yeah, but how?" Fitz whispered. He surveyed the restaurant. There were five other patrons. "It's not like we can get lost in the crowd."

"We're a bit conspicuous leaning down like this," Zee observed.

Fitz raised his head just enough to watch the Camaro back into a parking place four spaces down from Ben's car. He waited, hoping they wouldn't come in.

"Hey, guys. If they don't come in, why don't we just wait till the police get here?" Katía suggested.

"You've got a smart woman," Zee chuckled.

Fitz relaxed a bit of tension from his muscles. "They're just sitting in the car. Maybe they'll wait for us to come out."

"If they decide to come in, we're doomed," Ben said. "I've got an idea." He headed toward the counter.

"What are you doing?" Fitz called. He tugged his beard and ate M&Ms as he watched Ben place an order and hand the young man behind the counter a ten-dollar bill.

Ben hurried back to the group. "When this guy takes the burgers out to the goons, let's make a run for my car."

"Or we could hope that relieves them of the need to come inside. I say we wait for the police. They should be here any minute," Katía said.

Fitz checked his watch. It had been four minutes since Luna placed the call. Glancing over, he saw she was still on the phone.

"Katía's right again," Zee said. "If they do come inside, we can run out the other door."

"OK, let's wait. Ben, I think you just bought us the time we needed. Be ready to run to the other door, just in case," Fitz replied.

He watched as the worker took a bag and two drinks out to the Camaro. The confusion on the men's faces when he handed them the meals was priceless. Next, the driver's face turned dark and menacing.

"He must prefer hotdogs," Ben quipped.

The worker came back inside, and the men opened the car doors.

"Get ready," Fitz said. He waited to make sure they were coming in and not just trying to flush the park pals out of the building. The driver stood and shut the door.

"His finger's bandaged, and it looks like it's all there. I must not have shot it off," Katía observed.

Just before Fitz was going to say, "Run," the driver's head jerked to the side.

A second later Fitz heard it. "No, not sirens!"

The two men jumped back into the car and peeled out of the parking lot. The sirens continued to approach till three patrol cars pulled into the parking lot. Once the officers were out of their cars, the park pals went out to meet them.

"Sirens? Really?," Fitz griped as he approached one of the officers. "They heard you and ran."

"I'm glad it worked," the officer replied.

"If you had come in quietly, you could have apprehended them," Fitz said.

"If we had come in quietly, you and your friends might be dead by now," the officer countered, unfazed by Fitz's glare. "The woman who called this in told us when they got out of the car. That's when we hit the sirens."

Fitz sighed. "Oh. Sorry I came on a little strong."

Luna joined the group and stepped up to the officer. "Hi, I'm Luna Castillo. I'm the one who called it in, and I also got their photos." She held out her phone.

"Officer Renteria. It's nice to meet you," he said as he looked at the photos. "Perfect. I assume you're the one they abducted," he said as he approached Katía.

"Yes."

"I'm glad you escaped. Are these the men who abducted you?"

"That's them. I'll never forget their faces."

Renteria handed Luna her phone back. "Please text those photos to this number," he requested, handing her his card. "There's already a BOLO out for them. We'll add these photos to the others. We're going to catch them, ma'am," he said with assurance.

"I hope so. I'm tired of not being able to stay at my house," Katía replied.

The group stepped aside for one of the patrons to get by in his car. The three officers took statements from the park pals, then left.

"I seem to ask this a lot, but now what?" Zee asked.

"Obviously they know Ben's car," Fitz began. "We have to assume the one who hired them has a way of running the license plate, which means they'll figure out who you are and where you live."

"But they don't know we're staying there," Katía pointed out.

"One of us will have to keep watch at night," Ben said.

Fitz popped M&Ms into his mouth. "We also have to assume that soon those two won't be the only ones after us."

"I think it's time for you to stay at our house," Luna said. "Why risk staying at Ben's?"

"We come with critters," Ben noted.

"We don't mind. We keep our granddog sometimes. You and King are welcome, too," Luna directed to Zee.

"Thanks. I love pajama parties!"

Luna looked into Katía's eyes. "I really think you should consider postponing the wedding till this blows over."

"Oh, no! What time is it?" Katía gasped.

"Three fifty-seven," Zee said.

"I have to pick up Brian at the airport at five-thirty! We gotta get moving!"

Katía tugged on the door to Ben's Outback before he unlocked it. Ben whisked them to the church to pick up Katía's car.

"We'll have food when you get back," Ben said as Katía and Fitz jumped into her car.

"His flight had to arrive at rush hour," Fitz moaned as Katía drove at a crawl.

She handed Fitz her phone. "Text Brian that we're about fifteen minutes late."

After Fitz sent the text, Katía said, "We have one more day to catch these guys, then we're getting married."

"True. It would help if we had a plan, though."

Silence ensued as they racked their brains to come up with ideas. After a spell, Katía said, "That red Camaro is conspicuous. I'm going to count on the police catching them. That leaves Mr. or Ms. Big Fish."

"I hope you're right. I still think the key lies in figuring out what the real crime is that they are covering up by planting Harley and Nate at the scenes. If we knew what was stolen … or planted, we might could figure out who's behind it. … I hope Geraldine is still there."

He called the sheriff's office. "Hey, Geraldine, it's Fitz."

"I heard about Katía and y'all's close call at the Dairy Queen. Is she OK?"

"Yeah, she's good. I need a favor."

"Why am I not surprised?"

"Would you mind putting a bug in the ear of the detective who's covering the Nate Powell case? Suggest Nate was probably planted there to cover up another crime, I just don't know what it is yet. I think there's someone with a lot of power and influence behind these two cases. Something's happening that hasn't come to light. We need lots of eyes looking for it."

"So you want me to tell Detective Vitner he should be looking for a crime that doesn't appear to have been committed?"

"It sounds better the way I put it," Fitz replied.

"You're gonna have people questioning my sanity, Fitz. I'll let him know your theory, but you're gonna owe me big time."

"Just add it to my tab," Fitz chuckled.

After disconnecting, he told Katía, "As long as the detective isn't part of this crime ring, maybe he'll look for other possibilities."

Crawling through the snarl of cars in the airport pickup line, Katía said, "Keep a lookout for him."

"I don't know what he looks like."

"Oh, yeah."

Katía waved, snatching a spot along the curb after another car pulled out.

Fitz hopped out and watched as Katía ran and gave Brian a hug. *I should have trimmed my beard,* he thought as he waited to meet Brian, who was tall with the beginning of a receding hairline in his brown, wavy hair.

"Brian, this is Fitz, the love of my life. Fitz, my good friend, Brian."

"It's nice to meet you," Fitz said, extending his hand.

"You, too. I've heard a lot about you," Brian replied.

As Fitz loaded Brian's suitcase into the car, he said, "Take the front seat so you and Katía can catch up."

Katía added, "There have been some complications brewing. Have I got a story to tell you!"

CHAPTER 29

On the drive back from the airport, Katía filled Brian in on the robbery at the church, the unhoused guys arrests, the note on Fitz's car, the rocks through the windows, and finally her abduction and the episode at the Dairy Queen.

"You always did like to keep something stirring," Brian said. "But you didn't have to get so drastic just because I was coming into town."

Fitz chuckled. "So her mischief didn't start recently?"

"She's always been the mischievous sort," Brian replied.

"You can stop talking now," Katía laughed.

"Oh, but I want to hear more," Fitz urged.

"It didn't always involve near-death experiences. I understand she escalated to that level after meeting you."

"That part is true," Katía added. "Knowing Fitz has been rough on me."

"And you're going to marry him anyway," Brian said.

"I wouldn't have it any other way," Katía replied.

"Can I tell him about the banner?" Brian asked.

"If you must."

"It was our senior year," Brian began. "Katía had this brilliant idea. We snuck into the Candler library, pulled up the long banner that hung from the second mezzanine, and pinned felt letters onto it that read, 'Eccl. 12:12.'"

Fitz laughed but had no idea what Brian was talking about until Katía added, "It's a Bible verse that says, 'Of making many books there is no end, and much study is a weariness of the flesh.'"

Brian added, "It stayed up there for a number of years. I think the library staff liked it."

Fitz teased, "So you're not above breaking the law."

"Don't get any ideas," Katía said. "I'm sure the statute of limitations has run out on that one."

"Y'all sure had a whirlwind romance. Tell me about that," Brian said.

"It was another one of those near-death experiences," Katía began. "Three guys who were trying to kidnap wives for themselves tied me up and left me in a cave to die. Fitz came to save me but ended up in the same fix. It was in that cave that I realized I loved him. I think he made the same discovery. Over the next couple of months, we decided there was nothing to be gained by delaying the inevitable, so we're getting married Saturday, I hope."

"What do you mean, 'I hope'?" Brian asked.

"This whole people-trying-to-kill-us thing is throwing a monkey wrench into it."

Fitz pulled at his beard and dug out some M&Ms, grateful to be in the back where the others couldn't see.

"Do you really live in your car?" Brian asked. "If I'm being nosey, just tell me to shut up."

"I don't want to talk about it," Fitz said before he could catch himself. "Sorry, the situation back home has me stressed out. Katía says I'm supposed to be working on talking about things. Yes, I live in my car with my cat, Buffett."

Brian's next question caught Fitz off-guard. "That lifestyle fits with the minimalist trend these days. Do you enjoy it?"

Fitz puzzled over the question. "I've never thought about it that way. It's just been something Buffett and I do. It's all I've done since Buffett got me sobered up. I guess I have enjoyed it."

"Drastic changes are coming," Brian warned. "I don't think Katía will go for living in a car."

"No, we're living in my house," she said. "I think Fitz can learn to enjoy that, too. Buffett already has it down."

Katía was finally able to turn onto I-985, where the traffic eased. She parked in front of Luna's house.

"Uh-oh! I forgot to go by the church so you could get your car," Katía said.

"I didn't say anything since it's getting late. I hope the cats are OK, though," Fitz replied.

"I'm sure the bride needs some rest. I'll be happy to go with you to get the car and cats."

"I am tired," Katía replied.

Fitz knocked on the door and heard footsteps approaching.

"Come in," Luna chirped as she opened the door. "You must be Brian. It's nice to meet you! I've heard a lot about you."

"Uh-oh," Brian said as the three of them walked in.

"Buffett, Cotton, and Snow are tucked away in the laundry room," Luna explained.

"I was afraid they were still at the house. Thanks for picking them up," Katía said. "We were just wondering about them."

Fitz sensed something was wrong. "Where are Ben and Zee?"

"You noticed, huh?" Luna said. "They decided to stay at Ben's tonight so the three of you could each have a bedroom."

The suspicion that they had gone in hopes of confronting the abductors triggered the rage that had somehow remained in the background of Fitz's heart. He wanted those men to pay for what they had done to Katía with more than an injured finger. Fitz decided he had to go to Ben's.

"Brian is going to take me to the church to get my car," Fitz announced.

"We're letting the bride rest," Brian explained.

Katía handed over her key. "Y'all are so kind. See you when you get back." She gave Fitz a quick kiss.

When Fitz pulled into the church lot, Brian said, "So this is the famous Fitzmobile. I admire you for being able to manage living in your vehicle."

"Thanks, I think," Fitz replied. "Listen, I'm going to stay at Ben's tonight. Can you get back to Luna's, or do I need to lead the way?"

"Have GPS, will travel," he replied. "Are you coming over tomorrow? I'm hoping to get to spend some time with you."

"Yeah, I'll be there in the morning," Fitz replied.

Fitz drove two blocks past Ben's house and parked along the curb so the thugs wouldn't see his car if they showed up. He knocked on Ben's door and was greeted by the sound of barking dogs and footsteps. After a pause, Ben opened the door, gun in hand.

"You didn't think you could have my bachelor's party without me, did you?" Fitz asked, handing one of his extra Berettas to Zee.

"We were hoping to," Ben replied. "You're supposed to be staying at Luna's."

"Well, I'm not. I want to get my hands on those guys."

"Join the club," Zee chimed in. "They deserve a whippin' for kidnappin' Katía."

Fitz hung his jacket on the coatrack. "Do you have a plan, or are we just waiting to see what happens?"

"We were planning to take shifts watchin'," Zee answered. "I can get a few more hours beauty sleep now that you're here."

Fitz settled on the couch, heart and mind churning. *I hope they show up.* The sound of his phone startled him. It was Katía calling. "Hey."

"I can't believe you went to Ben's! You should have told me so I could have come with you."

"I wanted to help out here and wanted you to be able to relax."

"And just how am I supposed to relax, wondering what's happening over there? Did you ever think of that?"

Fitz pulled on his beard. "I'm sorry. We'll be careful."

"You'd better be. I don't want to have the wedding at the hospital. You can't get out of it by getting shot, you know."

CHAPTER 30

At ten o'clock, Ben stood up from the recliner and announced he was going to bed. He had insisted Fitz take the first watch, he the second, and Zee the third.

"Wake me up at one," Ben said. "Don't try to be a hero and stay up longer. Tomorrow's your wedding rehearsal, and you need to be awake."

"You do, too," Fitz pointed out.

"Never mind, I'll set an alarm."

"I'm gonna turn in, too," Zee said, and he and Ben went to bed.

Fitz was left in the den with his thoughts. *I should have spoken to Buffett before I left. He'll be OK, though. ... I should have brought him with me.* His stomach growled, reminding him he had not eaten. He went to the fridge to see what was available. The soft sound of a car door closing barely registered, but it was enough to bring Fitz to high alert.

He hurried to the front window and saw a Camaro parked on the road three lots down. His first instinct was to run out and start shooting, but he thought better of that. After turning off the lights, he went to alert Ben and Zee. They hopped out of bed still dressed in their clothes.

"They're earlier than I expected," Ben stated. "The plan is to surprise them and hold them for the police. Let's slip out the back and split up."

Fitz went to the left out the back door, with Ben and Zee taking the right. Fitz hurried to the front corner of the house, knowing he would remain concealed since they were approaching from the side Ben and Zee took.

Leaning his head out, he located one of the men but couldn't find the other. The one he saw was fumbling with something. It wasn't a gun. When the flame from a lighter flickered, Fitz knew what he was seeing: a Molotov cocktail.

His hand tightened on the Beretta as the rest of his body tensed. Time slowed. *Where is that other guy? I have to stop this one before he throws it.* Each second stretched out as Fitz's heart and mind raced. The lighter went out, and the man drew closer to Ben's front window.

Where is the other one? The man glanced toward the opposite corner of the house, giving away the other's location. The lighter flamed again, and Fitz knew he could wait no longer.

Stepping out, he yelled, "Drop it, or you're a dead man!"

He lit the Molotov cocktail, anyway. Fitz fired as he drew back to toss it. The man spun backwards, hitting the ground and slinging the flaming contraption across the grass. Fitz ducked back around the corner for cover, hoping Ben and

Zee had the other one subdued. Wanting to call out and ask, he held his tongue. He couldn't risk giving away their position. That's when he heard the last thing he wanted to hear.

"Drop it, or this one's dead! Now back away."

The other guy has Ben or Zee.

"Hey, you! You shot my man. Now I'm gonna shoot yours."

Highlighted by the fire in the grass, Fitz saw Ben with an arm around his throat and a gun to his head. The other criminal was behind him. The one he had shot was dragging himself toward the car. *I have to do something.*

Fitz stepped into view. "Why don't you let him go? I'm the one who shot your scumbag partner."

"Hey! You the scumbag!" The man yelled, waving his gun toward Fitz.

Ben seized the opportunity, grabbing the man's gun hand while he slammed his head into the guy's nose. Ben wrenched the man's arm around before slamming his elbow across his thigh. The gun fell to the ground, accompanied by a shriek from the gunman. Ben threw him down and drove his knee into the man's back, pinning him to the ground.

Fitz hurried forward as Zee came around the other corner. The one Fitz had shot drew a pistol. Before he could aim it, Fitz yelled, "Drop it! Now!"

The anger in that man's gaze was chilling as he stared Fitz down.

"I said, now!" Fitz called, Beretta leveled at his chest. The man tossed the gun to the side. Zee scooped it up.

"That was quite the move," Zee said to Ben.

"Thanks," Ben replied. "My ranger training paid off. You mind calling 911?"

"I thought you'd never ask," Zee quipped as he pulled out his phone.

Fitz stood over the man he had shot, aiming his gun at his head. "Who are you working for?"

The man didn't answer.

"Eddie, it will be a lot less painful if you go ahead and tell me." At Eddie's look of surprise, Fitz added, "Yeah, we know your names and where you live." When Eddie remained silent, Fitz said, "On the ground."

With Eddie on the ground and Fitz's gun still aimed at his head, Fitz pressed his foot down on Eddie's wounded shoulder. Eddie groaned.

"I'm not asking again. Who hired you?" Fitz pressed a little harder.

"I don't know." Eddie groaned.

Fitz pressed his foot down with half his weight.

Eddie yelped. "I don't know."

"So you just decided to do this on your own?" Fitz put his full weight down on Eddie's shoulder.

Eddie shrieked before mumbling, "OK. We got our orders from The Man."

Fitz let up a little. "What's his name?"

"That's all I know. He goes by 'The Man.'"

Fitz pressed a little harder. "Where can I find him?"

Amidst groans, Eddie said, "I don't know. I just get a text when he has a job."

"I need that number." Fitz growled.

"Won't do you no good. It's a burner. He only uses it once."

Fitz's anger burned like Ben's grass. He pushed down even harder on Eddie's shoulder.

After shrieking, Eddie managed, "I swear. That's the truth."

Fitz didn't let up on the pressure as he scrambled for a way to get answers from this guy before the police arrived. Finally, an idea surfaced. "How does The Man pay you?"

"He leaves cash in a dryer at the laundromat."

"You're not being very forthcoming. Which laundromat?"

"It's on Cleveland Highway."

"Cleveland Highway's a long road."

"Near the liquor store."

Fitz took his foot off Eddie's shoulder, and Eddie rolled onto his uninjured side.

Zee, who had finished calling in the incident, said, "That's a stubborn soul."

"He burnt my lawn," Ben griped, still holding Carl down.

"At least your house isn't burning down," Zee replied. "You can get up if you want to. I'll shoot 'im if he moves."

Ben stood up and stretched. "Thanks. I was getting stiff kneeling down like that."

Zee handed Ben his gun back, which he had picked up.

Fitz popped M&Ms into his mouth and chewed on them while his mind chewed on the new information he had. *So there's a middleman. He's the contact, and he contracts out the jobs. He's the next key in this mess.*

The sound of sirens preceded the flash of blue and red lights. Three sheriff's deputies pulled in just ahead of the ambulance. Standing behind their cars, the one in front ordered, "Drop your weapons and step back from the men on the ground."

The deputy narrowed his eyes when he noticed Zee holding three handguns. "You got enough weapons?" he quipped as they laid the guns on the ground, then stepped back about five yards. The deputy who had spoken kept an eye on them while the other two cuffed the men on the ground.

"Deputy Ray Kensington," the first officer introduced himself. "Somebody mind explaining what's going on here?" The other two deputies were already gathering the five handguns.

Ben relayed the story up to the deputies' arrival, leaving out the bit about Fitz stepping on Eddie's wounded shoulder but including Eddie's identifying 'The Man' as the one who had hired them. Fitz listened and watched the grass fire die out as Ben talked.

While Ben was telling the story, Deputy Benson called in the paramedics to tend to Eddie. They loaded him into the ambulance and took off before Ben finished.

Deputy Kensington asked if Fitz or Zee had anything to add. They shook their heads. "Are these the same two men who got away at the Dairy Queen earlier today?"

"That's them," Zee replied. "They've had a busy day."

"They'll have a busy night, too," Deputy Kensington chuckled.

Fitz, Zee, and Ben went inside after the deputies left.

"We're two steps closer to being out of this mess," Ben said, pouring himself a glass of tea. He held up the pitcher. "Any takers?"

"I worked up a thirst, too," Zee said.

Ben poured two more glasses.

Taking a sip, Fitz said, "I'm going to pay that laundromat a visit."

"I was afraid you'd say that," Ben replied.

"Can we at least finish our tea first?" Zee asked.

CHAPTER 31

Sitting at the counter in Ben's kitchen, Fitz pondered the possibility of going to the laundromat Eddie had mentioned. Considering the risks, he took a long drink of his iced tea before saying, "I think I should go alone."

Ben jumped in. "We know … it's going to be dangerous. That's exactly the reason you need us with you."

"Six eyes are always better than two," Zee added. "Just ask a spider."

"I thought spiders usually had eight eyes," Ben replied.

"That'd be even better," Zee winked.

"We're not getting Katía involved," Fitz growled.

"I didn't mean that," Zee said. "She's had enough for one day. Man, I just had a brilliant idea! You got any dirty laundry? We could take it with us so we look legit."

Ben gulped the rest of his tea and headed to the laundry room for his dirty clothes hamper. There wasn't much in it, so he grabbed a couple of towels on his way back. "Let's go," he said.

They loaded up in Ben's Outback and took off, leaving Snickers and King at the house. Ben pulled into the laundromat parking lot. No cars were there, but Fitz could see someone inside.

"Who'd be doing laundry this late at night?" Ben asked.

"Us, for one," Zee said. "Maybe he works the night shift and's gettin' it done before he goes to work."

Fitz noted that the man was putting clothes into his basket. "I think he's about to leave."

"That would be perfect timing," Ben said.

They got out, and Ben pulled the hamper from the back. "I forgot to bring detergent. This won't be very convincing."

"I bet they've got those little packets for sale inside. We'll just buy one of 'em," Zee suggested.

They went inside, and Ben put the hamper down at a washer. Just as Zee predicted, there was a vending machine with detergent, so he walked over to it. Fitz went straight to the dryers, looking for anything unusual and keeping an eye on the man who was folding his last pair of socks.

An "Out of Order" sign on one of the dryers was the only thing Fitz noticed. He tried to get a look inside the man's basket without his noticing. Clothes were all he could make out through the openings in the basket. The man left without so much as a glance in Fitz's direction.

Ben stopped before buying the soap. "Looks just like a laundromat."

"Check the washers," Fitz directed.

"He said it was a dryer, though," Zee pointed out.

Fitz returned to the dryer that was out of order and pulled it open. There was nothing inside. He gave his beard a tug and pulled out M&Ms. A door labeled "Office" caught his attention.

He walked up to the door and smelled smoke. Trying not to let on that he had noticed anything unusual, Fitz walked over to Ben and Zee. "Someone's in the office. I suspect we're on video."

"You think 'The Man's' hanging out in there?" Zee asked.

"I'm going to find out," Fitz said as he strode over to the door.

He knocked, and after a pause, the door opened. A large man with stringy black hair and stubble for a beard asked, "What?"

"Do you have change for a twenty? We need soap," Fitz asked.

"Use a card," the man said and closed the door.

Fitz slipped his foot forward, blocking the door just before it shut. "I don't have a card."

The man rolled his eyes as he pulled out a wallet. "I got fifteen I'll swap for your twenty."

While this exchange with the man played out, Fitz's mind was churning in the background. *He's hiding something. If Eddie was telling the truth, this guy could be responsible for Katia's abduction.* The man's behavior and Fitz's last thought combined and rage sparked.

Fitz pulled out his gun as he slammed his shoulder into the door, knocking the guy backwards a couple of steps.

"We need to talk," Fitz growled.

"I got nothin' to say to you," the man said as he dialed 911.

"I think you do," Fitz replied. "I think you're responsible for the abduction of my fiancé."

"You've lost your mind. I have no idea what you're talkin' about."

"I'll end your miserable life right now if you don't start talking."

"The only ones I'm talking to are the police. They should be here any second," the man grinned.

Fitz leveled his gun, ready to fire. Ben grabbed him by the arm. "No, Fitz. He's not worth it. We have to go."

As Ben dragged Fitz out of the laundromat, the man called out, "You'd better run, you coward."

Fitz jerked to get loose from Ben's grasp, but he held too tightly.

"Get in the car before you do something you'll regret for the rest of your life," Ben ordered.

"And don't shoot out a window," Zee added, holding the door open for Fitz.

"Should we wait on the police and tell them our suspicions?" Ben asked.

"He never pressed dial," Fitz said. "I would have heard the 911 operator answer. Let's go back in."

"No. If he's the kind of man we suspect he is, he'll be armed by now," Ben said, cranking the car and backing out.

"Better hurry," Zee said. "He's got a shotgun."

Ben punched the accelerator and careened onto the road.

"That was an exciting bachelor's party," Zee quipped.

While Fitz dug out some M&Ms, Ben said, "We have one more piece of the puzzle. I bet he leaves the cash in that dryer that's labeled out of order."

"I bet you're right," Zee replied. "He could stuff it in a pair of pants, and no one would notice."

"You'd make a good criminal, Zee," Ben laughed.

"Nah, that'd be too much stress for me, but I do have the mind for it."

"I hope the police follow up on Eddie's story about this place," Ben said.

"I hope the man leaves out the bit about Fitz pulling a gun on him if they question him," Zee added.

Fitz was quiet on the ride back to Ben's house. *I could wait till they're asleep, sneak out, and go back. The only way to find out what that man knows is to rough him up.*

He was trying to figure out how to go about that when Ben's voice broke into his thoughts. "If you're thinking what I think you're thinking, you could also get yourself killed."

Fitz scowled at him.

"It's a bad idea. Don't make me call Katía," Ben added.

"He can be a sneaky rascal," Zee said.

Fitz grunted and returned to his thoughts.

"You know the police won't go easy on you if they catch you attacking a man in his own place of business," Ben pointed out.

"You're suggesting we catch him away from the laundromat?" Fitz asked.

"No, I'm saying let the police question him and see what they get out of him. If he's not forthcoming, we can go to Plan B."

"What's that?" Zee asked.

"I have no idea," Ben laughed. "Our first order of business is to get Fitz some rest so he'll be fit to be a groom at the rehearsal tomorrow.

Ben parked the Outback in the garage, and they were greeted by two tail-wagging dogs as they entered the house.

As Fitz headed toward his bedroom, Ben said, "I mean it, Fitz. Don't go back tonight. That's just begging for problems."

"I get it," Fitz replied and stepped into the bedroom.

CHAPTER 32

A cold gray drizzle peppered the windshield as Ben drove to Laurel Park Friday morning. He had insisted on chauffeuring Fitz on this day before his wedding.

"I should have driven," Fitz grumped.

"What else are best men supposed to do?" Zee quipped. "We're supposed to take care of you and make sure you show up for the wedding."

Fitz had decided to call both Ben and Zee his best men for the ceremony. They were both on equal status in his heart. He replied, "I'll show up. What if Katía needs me to do something?"

"We're at your disposal all day," Ben replied. "I'm proud of you for not going back last night."

"Me, too," Zee added. "You gonna tell Katía about your bachelor party?"

Fitz tugged his beard and popped some M&Ms. "We have to tell her about the two goats who attacked. I think it's best to leave out our trip to the laundromat."

"Got it," Ben replied.

"She'll be glad to know the two that nabbed her are behind bars. … Well, technically I guess one's in the hospital with a sore shoulder," Zee said.

"The other one might have a broken elbow," Ben added.

While Ben parked, Fitz eyed the bathhouse. Out of habit, his mind began working through cleaning himself up when it dawned on him: *I won't ever have to do that again.* He tried to replace the sense of loss by thinking about Katía. *I'll get to wake up with her, instead.* The thought conjured a smile.

"You look chipper this morning," Ben noted.

"Probably thinking about his sweetie," Zee added.

Fitz was glad it was dark enough to hide the flush warming his cheeks. "You read my mind, but it's going to be hard to do a wedding with this crap going on. You should have let me rough that guy up to get some answers."

"I don't think they let people get married when they're in jail," Ben replied.

"That's true. You'd better put all of this on hold until after the honeymoon. Then we can start chasin' the rabbits," Zee suggested.

Fitz rubbed Buffett's harness, which was sitting in his lap. "I don't want Harley and Nate to have to stay in jail that long."

Headlights bobbing over the speed hump caught Fitz's attention. Looking directly at them, it took a minute before he realized something was wrong. "That's not Luna's car. Get behind the bathhouse!"

They jumped out, and Fitz got between Zee and the approaching vehicle, following as Zee hobbled. The vehicle was almost at the parking area when Fitz ducked behind the building.

"I'm sure they saw us," Zee said.

"Relax," Ben said. "It's a Park and Rec truck."

As they walked out from the bathhouse, the driver called out, "I hear congratulations are in order."

Fitz, Ben, and Zee approached the truck, and Fitz shook the driver's hand. "Thanks."

"In addition to congratulating you, I wanted to find out what time the rehearsal is. We're gonna get everythin' spic and span, but I don't want to be makin' a racket while you're rehearsin'."

"That's kind of you," Fitz answered. "It's at five-thirty. I hope you'll be home by then, though. I'd hate for you to work late on a Friday."

"Amen to that. I think this pea soup is gonna clear by mid-mornin'. You should have nice weather this evenin' and tomorrow. Congrats, again," he said as he drove off.

More headlights bobbed in the fog.

"That looks like Luna," Zee observed. "Better get the pups leashed up. She'll be rarin' to go."

Zee and Ben leashed up King and Snickers while Luna parked. Fitz hurried to embrace Katía as she got out.

"You missed me," she grinned.

"Yes, I did," Fitz said while looking inside the car.

"Oh, I left Buffett at the house. I didn't think he'd want to walk in this mess."

"You're probably right," Fitz replied, feeling a sting from not getting to see his cat. "I'll have to come by and get him later. Morning, Brian."

"Good morning! I trust you've ordered this drizzle to clear up before the rehearsal."

"No worries," Zee added. "We got it straight from Park and Rec that it'll be gone by noon."

"We're having a wedding tomorrow!" Luna chirped. "You're welcome to hang out at the house while I cook, Fitz. You and Buffett could spend some quality time together."

"Thanks. We'll see."

"Ben, Zee, this is my good friend Brian," Katía said.

After they had greeted each other, she took Fitz by the shoulders and looked into his eyes. "What's up, Fitz? Those guys showed up last night, didn't they?" Katía asked.

"Yeah, they did," Zee answered. "And they're both in custody now. You should have seen Ben take down the one that had him by the neck with a gun to his head. It could have been straight out of a movie."

I wish he hadn't told her that. Fitz said, "We're all OK. That's what matters."

"Uh, oh. What aren't you telling me?" Katía said, hands going to her hips.

"Busted," Zee laughed. "She can read you like a book."

"OK," Fitz added. "I shot one of the men in the shoulder. He's in the hospital, I suppose."

"Uh, huh. Ben?" Katía cut her eyes to him.

"It's all true," Ben answered.

"But is it all of the truth?" Katía countered.

Fitz popped M&Ms into his mouth before he could stop himself. *I'm busted.*

"Spill the beans, please," Katía said.

"OK. The guy I shot fessed up that a middleman hired them. Whoever is behind all of this paid him to contract with the men who abducted you."

Katía's eyes narrowed as she searched Ben and Zee's faces. "Let's hear the rest of the story, Zee."

"We paid the guy a visit but didn't learn anythin'. End of story," Zee said. "It was an amazin' bachelor's party."

Fitz glared at him, but Katía got tickled. "You guys have a warped idea of what a bachelor's party should be," she said.

"What about your bachelorette party?" Zee asked.

"We sipped hot chocolate and watched a movie. It was relaxing," Luna replied. "Now let's get moving. I have food to cook."

"And I have pork loins to marinate," Ben added.

Katía looped her arm through Fitz's and took his hand as they walked along the trail. "We're getting married tomorrow. Any cold feet?"

"None except that I'm worried about Harley and Nate. What's going to happen to them while we're on our honeymoon?"

Katía squeezed his arm and pulled him closer. "If it's that important and you think there's something we can do. … I guess we could postpone the honeymoon."

Fitz stopped in his tracks and turned to face Katía. "Really?"

"Really. If being here can help them, that's what we need to do."

Fitz pulled her to him and whispered, "That helps the cold feet."

"I'm not going to ask what you two are talking about, but I will point out it's cold and wet," Ben said, stopping about fifty feet down the trail.

"My ole joints are ready to get out of this," Zee added.

"OK, we're coming," Katía replied. She tugged Fitz back into motion.

"So you think this middle man is the key to figuring out who's really behind what happened to Harley and Nate?" Luna asked once Katía and Fitz had caught up and they were on their way again.

"I bet whoever is paying him had the same two men who nabbed Katía to abduct Harley and Nate and plant them at the crime scenes." Ben said. "They came after you and Fitz once we started poking our noses into their business."

"Please tell me you gave the police this middle man's name," Luna stated.

Fitz, Ben, nor Zee replied.

"Fitz?" Luna pressed.

"We don't know his name. The goon we captured just called him, 'The Man.'"

"We did tell them where he picks up his payments," Zee added.

"So they know where he is. All they have to do is arrest him and find out who's paying him," Luna said. "I hope this mess is over now, and we can focus on the wedding.

CHAPTER 33

As the park pals continued their walk around the trail that drizzly Friday morning, Fitz's anxiety ramped up. The stress, the changes to his routine, Buffett not being there all began to press in. Even as the light grew, darkness seemed to close around his heart. *I need some normalcy. I need my routine.*

By the time they reached the cars, his heart was pounding.

"You OK?" Katía whispered, drawing Fitz's mind back from the morass.

"I'm fine."

"If you're fine, you can ease up on the death grip," she replied.

He eased the pressure with which he was clenching her hand. "Sorry."

"What's wrong?" she whispered again.

"I need to get to my car and get Buffett. That's all."

Katía squeezed his hand. "I understand."

When they reached the cars, Katía asked, "Hey, Ben, would you mind taking Fitz back so he can get his car? He's going to come visit with Buffett for a while."

"I can just drop him by Luna's," Ben replied. "I'll be at his disposal if he needs to go anywhere."

"He needs his car. Besides, we have to go by the house to get ready for this evening. He might need something out of there."

"That makes sense," Ben said.

"Thanks," Fitz whispered before hugging Katía and kissing her.

After Ben parked in the garage, Fitz said, "I'll see you guys this evening," and walked to his car. He settled into the seat and sighed as he closed the door, relief washing over him. Leaning his head back, he relaxed in the familiarity of the Highlander. It felt like home. Glancing at the passenger seat, he realized he needed one more thing to be at home: Buffett.

Fitz pulled out of Ben's subdivision onto Cleveland Highway and drove north, looking forward to reuniting with his cat. Out of habit, he checked the rearview mirror and noticed a black Mustang pulling out of the subdivision about the same distance away that he would if he were tailing someone.

His suspicions grew as the car maintained a consistent distance about a tenth of a mile behind him. *Let's see if I'm imagining things.* He turned onto Honeysuckle, and the car followed.

Could be a coincidence. I'll take Wiley Road and loop back around to Cleveland Highway if it quits following me. What am I going to do if it is tailing me? I can't risk leading them to Luna's.

The car continued to follow Fitz down Wiley Road. *Let's see who's in that car. I'll get my phone ready for a photo.* He rolled up to the stop sign and waited for the car to catch up. While waiting, he entered 911 into his phone but didn't press dial before opening the camera app. He expected the driver of the car behind him either to stop a ways off, giving away their intentions, or to pull up behind him. The car approached at a creep but finally stopped behind Fitz. He turned and snapped a couple of photos of the two stout, bearded men behind him.

It looks like 'The Man' has new recruits. Now what? He pulled onto Clarks Bridge Road, his mind racing for an idea while his heart surged with anger. *I need to teach these guys a lesson.*

He pulled the Beretta from the console and tucked it under his thigh as he drove down the road that led to his favorite cul-de-sac by the lake. Stopping quickly at the end of the road, Fitz initiated the 911 call, tucked the phone under the seat, and jumped out, leveling the Beretta at the two men as they pulled up.

"Get out with your hands up," Fitz yelled. Both doors opened, and the men got out. The one on the passenger side raised his hands, holding a knife by the tip. Fitz recognized the hold on the knife too late to fire. He jumped to his right as the knife flew at him.

The knife missed, but Fitz's reaction opened up a sufficient window for the driver to tackle Fitz and pin him to the ground. His face digging into the asphalt, Fitz saw the other man approaching with a 2x4.

"What do you want?" Fitz growled.

"We're your teachers, and you're gonna learn a lesson," the one with his knee on Fitz's back answered as he pulled the gun from Fitz's hand. "First, you shouldn't play with guns. You could get yourself hurt."

The man holding the 2x4 laughed. "Good one."

"Thanks," the first one chuckled. "You wanna learn your lesson lyin' down or standin' up? It don't matter to us."

I have to keep these guys talking till the police get here. "What lesson are you teaching today? If I know, I can learn it quicker."

The one with the 2x4 smacked it into his palm. "The Man said you'd figure it out. Get up so I can knock you down."

"Who's the man?" Fitz asked.

"None of yo' business," the driver said. "Get up." He moved his knee from Fitz's back and tugged him to his feet by his collar. The driver stepped back, and the 2x4 collided with Fitz's left shoulder, knocking him back to the ground.

Holding his shoulder, Fitz said, "You guys aren't very good teachers. I have no idea what this is about. How about telling me before you pound it into me."

"The boss said you'd know. That's all we need," the driver said.

"You mean you'd risk going to jail just because this boss tells you to go beat up someone?" Fitz asked. "That's not very bright. I think a teacher would know better."

"Shut up and get up." The driver pulled Fitz to his feet, and the 2x4 collided with Fitz's back. He hit the asphalt again, gasping for breath.

"Hey, Joe, let's do this guy like a pig on a rotisserie. We'll hit all four sides.

The guy with the 2x4 laughed. "I like it."

"Get up and take your lesson like a man," the driver demanded.

Fitz tried to push himself up but failed. The driver grabbed his collar and pulled. "Come on, ole man."

Fitz worked to present his right side toward the 2x4 and waited for the hit. Nothing happened, and he noticed the driver looking up the road. The sound of an approaching vehicle registered.

"We gotta go," the driver said just before the 2x4 knocked Fitz to the ground again.

Fitz rolled to make sure he wouldn't get run over. The driver whipped the vehicle around just as a patrol car appeared. The deputy blocked the road with her vehicle and hit the blue lights.

The Mustang bounced over the narrow ditch and tore through a yard before regaining the road as it sped away. Fitz lay on his back, watching the scene play out. As the deputy's car approached, he tried to get to his feet but gave up.

Deputy James got out and yelled, "Don't move."

Fitz noticed her eyeing the gun. *At least they didn't get my Beretta.* He listened as she radioed for an ambulance.

"Fitz?"

"Yeah," he moaned.

"Now what have you gotten yourself into?" Deputy James asked as she donned gloves and picked up the gun.

She bagged it, placed it in her car, and approached Fitz.

"Those two guys said they were going to teach me a lesson," Fitz said with a cough. "Oh, that hurt."

"Anything broken?"

Fitz lifted his left arm. "I can move it. That one, too," he added after lifting his right arm.

"Can you tell me what happened here?"

With a few groans, Fitz went through the whole story, including the two men last night, their trip to the laundromat, and the men following him to the cul-de-sac.

He ended with, "I believe the man at the laundromat is the one hiring the thugs."

His explanation was followed by the blare of a siren as an ambulance approached.

"If you'll get my phone from under the driver's seat, I can show you a photo of the two guys."

Fitz opened his phone to the photos and handed it back to Deputy James. She texted them to herself before returning the phone to Fitz.

The paramedics hurried out of the ambulance to assess Fitz.

"I don't think anything is broken, but I believe you need some x-rays to be sure," one of the paramedics said.

As they helped Fitz walk to the gurney, Deputy James said, "I'll let Katía know you're headed to the hospital."

CHAPTER 34

Fitz heard Katía's comforting voice long before she got to his ER bay. Not that she was using a comforting tone, but he was glad she was there.

"Where is he? Show me his room!"

A nurse stepped aside for Katía, who flew through the door. "What happened? Are you OK?"

She pulled down the sheet and eyed the budding bruises and swelling in his arms. Her gaze was so intense, Fitz felt he was back in x-ray. "I'm fine. Nothing's broken. They're finishing up the paperwork, then I can get out of here."

Katía kissed him and said, "Diann said you got a picture of them. They've attacked the wrong person, and I'm not letting them get away with it."

"I'm sure their mugshots will show up. They seem the type to be frequent flyers at the jail," Fitz said. "I just wish I'd gotten their tag number."

"Diann said she got that."

Fitz took her hand. "Thanks for coming to see me."

She nuzzled her face into his neck, being careful of his arms. "You're quite welcome."

"You're all set to go," the nurse announced as she entered the emergency room bay. "You can expect to be sore for a few weeks. I'd use acetaminophen for pain. NSAIDS are likely to cause more bleeding for the first few days. Any questions before we let you go?"

"No, but thanks for taking care of me," Fitz replied.

She handed him his shirt. "Here's your paperwork. As soon as you're dressed, you can go."

When Fitz discovered his arms hurt if he reached behind his back, Katía helped him get his shirt on.

"Good thing we're getting married tomorrow. You're going to need round-the-clock care," Katía smiled.

"I'm glad you're willing to be my nurse."

Ben and Zee charged into the emergency waiting room as Fitz and Katía walked out of the treatment area.

"Man, you look awful," Zee announced.

"Thanks," Fitz replied.

"You OK?" Ben asked.

"I'll make it," Fitz answered.

"What can we do?"

"You can go get Fitz's car," Katía replied. "I don't want him trying to drive. His arms are beat up badly."

"You got the key?" Ben asked.

Fitz dug into his pocket. "Uh, oh. I left it in the ignition. It's at that cul-de-sac where we had the picnic after the lunatic doctor take-down.."

"There probably aren't many car thieves prowlin' that road. I expect it'll be OK. We'll go fetch it," Zee said.

It was lunchtime when Katía parked in front of Luna's house. Fitz moaned as he pushed the car door open. He hurried in to see Buffett, who greeted him with meows, purrs, and leg rubs. As soon as he sat on the couch, Buffett jumped into his lap.

"I missed you, too," Fitz said, stroking Buffett's back while Buffett nuzzled his chin.

"The soup's heating up and salads are in the fridge. I trust you're hungry," Luna announced.

Brian walked into the room. "There's never a dull moment around here. How are you, Fitz?"

"I'll make it," Fitz answered.

Before the soup was ready, Ben and Zee walked in. Zee handed Fitz the keys as he said, "That's a sweet-drivin' vehicle. You sure you don't wanna trade?"

Fitz cut his laugh short. "Ouch."

"I'm tired of these creeps interfering with your wedding," Ben said. "I'd love to get ahold of these last two."

"Forget about them until after the wedding," Luna said, hands on hips. "We have to make these next two days special, and I don't mean get-beat-to-within-an-inch-of-your-life special. You're allowed to talk about it, but there'll be no more going after these creeps. Now have a seat and prepare for my world-renowned ham soup."

"Man! I could eat this every day!" Zee said after his first bite.

Luna got down to business. "What else do we need to do before the rehearsal?"

"We'll need to go to the house to get ready," Katía said. "I didn't think to bring our clothes."

"I can iron anything that needs pressing," Luna offered.

"I went ahead and did that. I wanted as few chores as possible left for this weekend," Katía replied.

"I have to put the asparagus casserole together," Luna added.

"I have to get the pork loins grilled," Ben said.

"Good. None of us have time for anything dangerous," Luna said, sounding relieved.

"What in the world do you think's up with these guys?" Zee asked.

Fitz noticed the scowl Luna gave him. "Obviously someone doesn't want their exploits exposed," Fitz said. "We know who the little guys are but have no idea who's really behind all this."

"We don't know what they're behind, either," Ben observed.

"This is the craziest thing I ever heard of," Zee said. "Why act like two guys broke into a place but didn't steal anythin'? Don't make a bit of sense."

"You're right, it doesn't make any sense," Ben replied. "What if we've been thinking about this the wrong way? What if the whole point of the crimes was to get Harley and Nate locked up?"

"Why would someone want to do that?" Katía asked.

"They had a beef with them?" Ben said.

"Like owin' 'em money," Zee suggested.

"Yeah, or stealing some drugs," Brian added.

Fitz stirred his soup, pondering what they were saying. "So far we haven't heard any mention of there being any drug connections or gambling issues with Harley or Nate. From what I know of them, they just keep to themselves and do a bit of drinking. There has to be another motive."

"Shall we pay the laundromat king another visit?" Ben asked. "We could be a little more persuasive this time."

"No. Absolutely not," Luna said. "From now through tomorrow, all we're doing is wedding stuff. You and Zee can play with that guy after we send Fitz and Katía off."

Ben grinned. "Please. It would just take a few minutes. We could stop in while Fitz is on his way to Katía's. Just Zee and me."

Luna rolled her eyes. "I thought you had a grill to tend to. We need food for the rehearsal dinner, you know."

"Yes, ma'am," Ben replied.

Fitz caught Ben's attention and gave a quick nod.

When Katía's phone pinged, she scrunched her eyebrows as she read the notification.

"That bad?" Zee asked.

"Winslow's airing another interview. I'd better listen in." She got up to leave the table.

"Wait, I'd like to hear it, too," Ben said.

"Do y'all mind?" Katía asked.

"Just stay put and turn 'im on. Let's hear his latest rant," Zee added.

Katía opened the WDUN stream to find the interview in progress with Winslow speaking.

"We know of three serious crimes committed by the homeless riffraff in our community within the last week, one in my own restaurant. They even robbed my church, taking thirty-six hundred dollars that was meant for a shelter to help them out. Who knows how many other crimes they have committed? I bet most of the robberies in the city were done by them.

"It's time we do something about this. It's time for them either to leave or to be put in jail where they belong. I believe the vast majority of Gainesvillians would like to have the city cleaned up so it's a more reputable place.

"I'm calling on the citizens of Gainesville to show up and back me at the next council meeting—where I will propose once again that we direct the police to actively enforce the vagrancy laws and arrest anyone in violation. The meeting has been called for next Thursday at seven p.m. Please be present and show your support. Thank you very much."

Fitz clenched both fists as anger surged. His jaw tightened, and he gave his beard a tug as what he had just heard registered. He left the table and paced in the den.

Katía caught up with him. "You can't let him get to you like this. I know he's a jerk, but he's just one man. The city will rally against him just like they did last time."

Fitz battled with whether to tell Katía what he had just figured out. It registered that she was rubbing his back, which was terribly sore from the 2x4 smack. He pulled away.

Katía's eyes widened, "Oh, I'm sorry. I forgot about your back hurting."

The battle continued raging in Fitz's heart. He wanted to tell her but was afraid she wouldn't believe him, or even worse, would be hurt by the realization.

"Talk to me, Fitz. What's wrong?"

"I know who's behind all of this," he blurted out.

"What do you mean?"

"How could Winslow Johnston know how much money was stolen from the church? That's the second time he has said it."

"I thought we decided he just made it up."

"I don't think so. He's the one orchestrating all these 'robberies' in order to drum up support for his proposal."

"No way," Katía said, covering her mouth. "Wait, I can see it now. He is enough of a scoundrel to do it."

"We need some proof before we can accuse him and getting it will be dangerous."

CHAPTER 35

Fitz and Katía returned to Luna's dining room and joined the others as they finished their lunch.

"Everything OK?" Luna asked.

"Fitz figured out who's behind these crimes, even the church robbery," Katía answered.

"Well, don't keep us in suspense," Zee said.

"It's Winslow Johnston," Katía announced.

"Really? What makes you think that?" Ben asked.

"He has said how much was stolen from the church twice on the radio. Even I don't know how much was taken," Katía replied.

"That weasel! He does seem to be a scumbag," Ben said. "So you're thinking the church robbery is connected to whatever's going on with Harley and Nate?"

Fitz nodded. "I think it's all part of his effort to rid the city of residentially-challenged folks."

Zee swallowed his last bite of cornbread. "That does make sense, but it's an awful low thing to do, even for a politician."

Brian added, "That's just crazy, but you hear of politicians doing stuff like this more often than you'd expect."

Luna pulled out her phone. "Should I call Gainesville City Police or the sheriff's office?"

"Hold on. We need proof before we call it in. So far all we have is speculation," Fitz said.

"Let's give them your theory and let them find the proof," Luna said.

"They won't pursue it unless they believe it's credible, especially with Johnston being a councilman," Fitz added.

Luna huffed. "Well, he'll just have to get away with it till after the wedding."

Katía stood. "We'd better get going. It's already one-thirty."

"How long does it take to get ready?" Zee asked.

"Zee!" Luna scolded. "You never comment on how long a bride needs to get ready."

"Oh. Sorry." Zee replied.

"I need to get my things together," Brian said.

"You'd better stay here tonight, don't you think?" Luna said. "They might still target your house. Brian's welcome to get ready here."

"Can't they target the house during the day just as well?" Brian asked.

"Yeah, but it's a lot less likely," Ben replied. "Zee, we've got some grilling to do."

"Yes, sir," Zee said, pushing his chair back.

"We'll see you at the park," Luna waved as the others walked down the driveway.

Fitz caught up to Ben. "Are you thinking what I'm thinking?"

"Probably," Ben said. "We need to do a little laundry right quick."

"Right. I'd better tell Katía," Fitz said.

Fitz hurried over to Katía, who was about to get into her Prius. "Ben, Zee, and I are going to stop by the laundromat and ask that guy if Johnston's the one paying him."

"Do you think that's a good idea? You're already hurt."

"That's the only way I know to find out."

Katía looked deeply into his soul and said, "I'm coming with you."

"Oh, no," Fitz moaned, knowing that arguing would be pointless.

Pulling into the laundromat parking lot, Fitz noticed two cars. He parked three spaces away from Ben and surveyed inside the building, seeing four people. Katía pulled in between him and Ben.

As Fitz was getting out, he noticed a man looking around. It seemed he was checking to see if anyone was watching. He was near the dryer that had been labeled "Out of Order." *He's picking up his payoff.* Sure enough, the man pulled something from the dryer and exited the building.

Whipping out his phone, Fitz snapped a photo. He took another one of the car as it pulled out.

"What are you doing?" Katía asked.

"Getting some leverage," Fitz said. "That guy just picked up a package from the dryer that's out of commission."

"Brilliant," Zee said. "Let's find out what this guy has to say."

"Got your gun? Fitz asked Katía.

"I do," she grinned.

Fitz led the group into the building and went straight to the office door. He knocked. There was no response, so he knocked louder. Nothing happened.

"Does anyone have paper and a pen?"

Katía pulled a pen and notepad out of her purse and handed them to him.

Fitz wrote, "Talk to me or I'll send the photos of the recent pickup to the police," then slid the paper under the door. Fitz heard footsteps, and after a few seconds the door opened.

"Come in, my friends," said the same scraggly-looking man they had seen before.

The group filed into his little office, and the man shut the door.

Fitz began, "I'm not asking you for any information. Nobody will be able to say you're the source. I'm just going to give you a name, and I want you to nod or shake your head. Got it?"

The man sat down at his desk and whipped a handgun from the drawer. Fitz, Ben, and Katía responded by drawing their weapons.

"Like I said," Fitz resumed. "All you have to do is nod or shake your head and your profitable arrangement won't be exposed." Fitz could tell he was weighing the possibility of shooting all three of them before they could shoot him. Finally he nodded and lowered his gun.

"Winslow Johnston," Fitz said.

The man glared at him, sitting silently. Fitz moved his finger to the trigger. "I'm not waiting all day." Fitz could tell he was weighing his options. He gave a single nod.

"Thanks. We'll let you get back to business," Fitz said and motioned the others to leave the room. He backed through the door, making sure the man didn't have second thoughts about shooting.

When they gathered around the cars, Ben said, "What are the chances he was lying?"

"Pretty high," Zee replied. "I'm not sure we know any more than we did before we got here."

"We know one thing," Fitz said. "He's a calculating soul."

"But what's he calculating?" Katía asked. "Is telling us Johnston's behind this an attempt to steer us away from the real culprit, or is he telling the truth in order to get the heat off himself?"

"His type are slippery. That's how they survive," Zee said. "I'm kind of leanin' toward Katía's second idea."

"True. He knows we're onto him. If he can turn the attention to Johnston, maybe the police will forget about his involvement," Ben suggested.

"If Johnston's not involved at all, he'll have us on a wild goose chase that leads to a dead end," Fitz said.

"So you're sayin' we did all that for nothin'," Zee griped.

"Not at all," Fitz replied. "I'm betting he was telling the truth and hoping we'll think he was lying. Like you said, he's slippery."

"If it's true, then how do we catch a councilman?" Ben asked. "He'll be even slipperier than this guy."

CHAPTER 36

Katía led Fitz into the house to get ready for the rehearsal. Setting her purse down, she asked, "What's this?" as she picked up a small, wrapped gift.

After Katía's abduction, Fitz had forgotten about the necklace he bought for her. He came up from behind and wrapped his arms around her. "Something I thought you might like."

"Can I open it?"

"Of course."

She unwrapped the box to find the necklace of carved animals. "I don't know what to say. It's gorgeous! I'm wearing it tonight!" Spinning around in Fitz's arms, she kissed him. "Thank you."

"You're more than welcome."

"I'm going to get ready so I can put it on!"

While Katía showered, Fitz sat on the couch with Buffett in his lap, stroking his fur and pondering the situation to the soothing sound of the cat's purr. *It makes sense that Johnston's behind this. He keeps using this stuff in his quest to get rid of us. Without the city suspecting that the residentially-challenged are committing a lot of crimes, there would be no reason to support him. Would he stoop so low as to rob his own church, too? I need more proof than the word of a scumbag. I bet that's what he was thinking on so hard before he answered. He knew his answer would not be enough for us to go after Johnston.*

Fitz's eyes popped wide when Katía walked into the room wearing towels around her body and hair.

"You haven't showered yet?" she asked.

Fitz shook his head. Katía grinned, walked over, kissed him and said, "After tomorrow, I won't need a towel." With a wink, she said, "Hop up and get ready."

Fitz watched her walk out of the room before shooing Buffett out of his lap. "I have to get ready for the rehearsal," he explained to Buffett.

He tried to wrestle his mind off Katía and back to Johnston. *If he's the one, how can I prove it?* The solution crystalized.

Checking his watch, he saw it was just 2:30 p.m. He felt his heart rate speed up. *I have to hurry!* Fitz called Serena Granger at the Times.

"Hey, Serena, it's Fitz."

"Hey, Fitz, what's up?"

"I need you to put out an online story for me."

"Fitz, it's two-thirty on a Friday afternoon. I was about to head out."

"Please. It won't take long."

"Good grief! I hope this is important."

After Fitz got off the phone with Serena, he called Ben.

"Hey, Ben, I need you to meet me at Katía's church in an hour."

"I'm getting ready to put the pork loins on. I can't."

"Let Zee watch the pork loins. I need you to pick up a couple of security cameras, on your way."

Disconnecting the call, Fitz walked into the hallway. "Katía?"

She peeked her head through the doorway. "Yeah?"

"Do you have a firesafe?"

"No, do you think we need one?"

"That's OK. I'll just use my lockbox."

"For what?"

"Nothing. Wait, I need a key to the church."

"OK." As she handed the key out the cracked-open doorway, she asked, "What do you want this for?"

"To set a trap. I have to hit the shower."

Fitz hurried through the shower and donned the new khaki pants and hunter green polo Katía had bought for the occasion. He told Katía he'd be back in a few minutes, then headed to the church. He unpacked his spare Berettas and ammunition from the lockbox and buried all of it carefully under the clothes that had covered the lockbox.

He strained to hold the lockbox with one hand and a thigh while he unlocked the church door. Just as he pushed the door open, he heard a car pull up. Ben joined him.

"Care to explain what we're doing that's more important than my pork loins?" Ben asked.

"We need proof if we're going to implicate Johnston. Serena's running an article that says an anonymous donor has restored the money the church lost in the robbery and that the offering box is back in place. We're setting the church up to look like they're back in business with the offering. I'm hoping he'll take the bait and rob again."

"You do have your moments of brilliance, don't you? Let's get moving. You have a wedding rehearsal to make."

They got to work setting up the security cameras in inconspicuous locations.

"I don't suppose you brought a computer," Ben said.

Fitz was flummoxed. "I didn't think about that."

"That's why I brought this one," Ben said, pulling one of his old laptops out of the bag.

With the cameras up and running, Fitz walked into the church and up to the lockbox to make sure the cameras would see an intruder.

"Perfect," Ben announced. "Now we have to get you to the rehearsal. I hope Zee didn't mess up the pork loins."

When Fitz pulled into the parking place five minutes late, he was grateful to see that Luna and Brian had not arrived yet. Katía hurried over and gave him a kiss as he got out.

"I can't believe the time is finally here!" she said.

"It's a good thing you two didn't have a long engagement," Ben teased. Turning to Zee, he asked, "How did the pork loins come out?"

Zee put his fingertips to his lips, made a kissing sound, and said, "Pure perfection."

Katía took Fitz's arm. "Exactly what did you do at the church?"

Fitz explained the trap they had set. "I hope he takes the bait."

"Me, too. That's a clever idea. I just wish we had more time for him to bite before we leave for the honeymoon. I could tell one of the church members what's going on so they can keep an eye on it." She paused and looked out over the lake. "Or I guess we agreed we could stay here and honeymoon later."

Her disappointment hit home. "What if we give Ben a key and have him keep a check on things?" Fitz asked.

Katía smiled. "Really? That would be great!"

"I'm sure he wouldn't mind," Fitz said.

"Wouldn't mind what?" Ben asked.

"Keeping an eye on the church cameras while we're gone," Fitz explained.

"I'd be honored," Ben said. With a bow he added, "Ben's Surveillance at your service."

Luna and Brian arrived, and Brian guided everyone through lining up, then walked them through the ceremony.

It took a minute to decide where to position Buffett, Snickers, and King. In order to balance out the attendants, Katía had asked Shirley, from the church, to be a bridesmaid. Shirley got the honor of managing Buffett's leash.

Once everyone understood how to go through the ceremony, Brian said, "Let's end with a prayer. Dear loving God, we are grateful for your gift of love that undergirds each of us. We are especially thankful for the love you have given Katía and Fitz for each other. We pray you will walk with them each day of their lives and fill them with the joy of your presence. Amen."

Looking up from the prayer, Fitz spied Winslow Johnston on the walking path with his dog, Rip. He had apparently been waiting for them to finish the prayer before walking up.

"Pastor, I understand two congratulations are in order. Congratulations on the wedding and congratulations on the church getting the stolen money back."

Fitz was glad he had told Katía about the trap so she wouldn't be caught off-guard.

"Thank you, Winslow. We didn't exactly get the money back. Someone replaced it."

"Well, it amounts to the same thing. Are you at liberty to say who made the donation?" Winslow asked.

"I'm sorry, but they want to remain anonymous," Katía replied. "At least we're back in business for the shelter offering. I've already put out another donation box."

"I see. Well, it's good news all the same. I look forward to celebrating your wedding tomorrow. See you then." Winslow gave Rip's leash a tug, pulling him away from sniffing Snickers and King. "Come on, Rip."

After Winslow had walked out of earshot, Katía asked, "Am I the only one who thinks that was eerie?"

"It was a creepy coincidence," Ben added. "I wanted to punch him but restrained myself."

"I'm proud of ya," Zee said. "Such self-control."

"You don't think he was close by enough to have heard us talking about the trap, do you?" Katía whispered.

"I hope not. I didn't notice him lurkin' about," Zee said.

"Trap? What do you mean?" Luna asked.

Katía explained the plan to lure the councilman into the church.

"What makes you so sure it's him? I thought you said all we had was conjecture," Luna pointed out.

All four of the other park pals looked away. Fitz stared across the lake for a moment before sheepishly explaining how they had stopped by the laundromat, and the man there admitted Johnston was behind it all.

Luna's hands went to her hips, and Fitz braced for a scolding.

Luna relaxed a bit before saying, "I can't believe you did that. Even more, I can't believe it's Johnston behind all of this. How could he do such things? Do you really think he'll break into the church again?"

"We're hoping so," Ben replied.

"You know what else you've done, don't you?" Luna asked, hands back on her hips.

"What?" Fitz asked.

"You've put another unhoused person at risk of being knocked over the head."

CHAPTER 37

The group convoyed to Luna's house for the rehearsal dinner. The sun was showing off its artistic skills in the western sky.

"Look at that, Buffett," Fitz said. "I wonder if you ever pay attention to the sunset. Is that something cats do?"

"Meow."

"I'm glad. I guess you just see it in gray scale, though."

"Meow."

"Our lives are about to change drastically. Actually, I guess they already have, haven't they?"

"Meow."

"We haven't slept in the car for a while now. I trust you'll be able to adapt to living in a house."

"Meow."

"Good. I think I'll be able to adapt, too. If we get antsy, we can always go for a drive." Fitz reached over and rubbed Buffett's head. "You're such a good cat."

"Meow."

"OK, I'll give you some treats when we get to Luna's. You might even get a bite of pork loin."

"Meow!"

Fitz parked along the road at Luna's and placed six cat treats on the seat. Rather than harnessing Buffett, he scooped him up and carried him in. He set him on the floor, and Buffett trotted off to greet Cotton and Snow.

"It looks like they're going to get along just fine," Luna observed.

"Yeah, so far Buffett doesn't seem to be having any problems with the transition," Fitz replied.

"You're going to make it, too," Luna added, patting his arm. Fitz winced, and Luna added, "Sorry." She announced, "OK, everybody, the food's ready. We'll let the bride and groom serve themselves first. Katía, will you say a blessing?"

"I'm going to defer that honor to Brian today," she replied.

Brian said, "Let's pray. Blessed are you, O Lord our God, King of the universe. You created us and gave us life. You provided this food to nourish us and gave us the gift of your Spirit to sustain us. We thank you for all these gifts and especially for the gift of love that undergirds life with joy. Amen."

As they lined up to get their plates, Fitz wrapped an arm around Katía and hugged her to him.

"What's that for?" she asked.

"Just feeling happy. Buffett and I had a good talk on the way over."

She leaned into him.

"OK, let's move it along. There's hungry folks back here," Zee teased.

"Zee!" Luna scolded.

During dinner, the talk turned to tomorrow's wedding. Luna put Carlos in charge of getting Brian to the park so she could be with Katía. "Ben, you and Zee are in charge of getting Fitz there. Is it OK if he just leaves his car at your house during the honeymoon?"

"That's fine with me," Ben replied.

"We'll stop by my house … oops, our house and change before we drive to St. Simons. Are you sure you're OK with the cats staying here?"

"I'm happy to keep them," Luna answered. "They've just made themselves at home."

"Do you think anyone will step into our trap?" Zee asked.

"I guess we'll find out in the morning," Ben replied.

The next morning, Ben opened the door to Fitz's room. "Wake up. It's wedding day!"

Fitz flung off the covers, and they landed on Buffett, who was nestling beside him. "Sorry, Buffett."

He showered and met Ben and Zee in the kitchen. "Let's go check the video."

"How about some breakfast and coffee first? Since the church has wi-fi, I set it up so I can see it from here," Ben said.

"What are we waiting for, then?" Fitz replied.

Ben booted up the computer and accessed the camera footage, Fitz and Zee each hovering over a shoulder. Ben fast-forwarded until he saw movement.

"I can't believe it! Somebody actually took the bait!" Ben said. He stopped the video and backed up. The three men watched as a foot, a leg, then a whole person appeared on camera. The image was followed by a second person right on their heels.

"There's two of 'em." Zee observed.

They watched the tape tell the tale of the two people entering the sanctuary, prying open the lockbox, pulling out a paper, and looking surprised. They ran out of the sanctuary and out of the building, disappearing from view.

"That was priceless!" Ben laughed.

"I want to watch it again," Zee chuckled. "See if you can zoom in on their faces when they read the note."

"We do need to find clear enough images to identify them," Fitz added, "But they're obviously not part of the residentially-challenged community."

Ben zoomed in on the shot where they pulled the paper from the box. It was a note that read, "Gotcha!" The grainy image was hard to see until Ben enhanced it.

"Wow!" Ben said. "Both of them? I can't believe it."

"We gotta tell Katía," Zee said.

"Let's not bother her with this," Fitz said, anger quickening his heartbeat. "Just let her focus on getting ready. I'll meet a deputy at the church."

"Wrong," Ben said. "We'll meet a deputy at the church. I have clear instructions to keep an eye on you and make sure you get to the church on time and without getting beat up."

Fitz called the sheriff's office. "There's been another break-in at St. Luke's United Methodist Church. This time the burglars were caught on video. Can a deputy meet us there in about fifteen minutes?"

Ben drove them to the church, where he copied the video and two enhanced still shots onto a flash drive. He was just finishing when Fitz heard a car pull up.

Deputy James walked into the church. "It's really rare to have two robberies at the same church this close together."

"There might have been a little encouragement," Zee said.

She gave Zee an incredulous look. "Where's Katía?"

"She's getting ready for the wedding," Ben answered.

"Of course, I should have thought of that," Diann replied. "Let's see what you've got here."

Fitz showed her the pried-open lockbox before leading her to the office. "Ben will walk you through the video footage we captured."

Ben clicked on the play button, turned the computer to face Diann, and leaned back in the office chair. When it reached the point where the faces were the clearest, he paused it and enhanced the image.

"Oh, my!" Diann gasped. "This is bad."

Ben held up a flash drive. "I made a copy for you."

"Actually, I'm going to need the computer. I'll get this to the lab so they can verify its authenticity. We can't proceed until then. I also need the three of you to keep this quiet. No blabbing to the community or posting on social media."

"Yes, ma'am," Zee said.

Ben slid the flash drive into his pocket. "I guess I can do without my computer for a while. Any idea when I can pick it up?"

"Once the lab has verified the footage, we'll let you know," Diann replied.

"I believe you will find that these two are behind the Harley Smith and Nate Powell crimes, too. They had their minions knock them out and place them at the scenes to help stoke their war on the residentially-challenged community," Fitz said.

"I was afraid you were going to say that," Diann replied.

"If it helps, I know where these guys will be at eleven-thirty today," Fitz said.

Diann slowly grinned. "That would be epic, but I hate to mar your wedding."

"Just wait till it's over," Fitz said with a grin. "It'll be a nice wedding present for Katía."

CHAPTER 38

Fitz, Ben, and Zee watched as Diann drove away from the church. Checking his watch, Fitz felt an adrenaline surge. It was 8:45 a.m., less than three hours until his wedding.

"We have to go!" he said. "Do you mind driving me by a barber shop on the way?"

Ben's and Zee's jaws dropped. "Say that again," Ben said.

"I have decided to trim up this scraggly beard."

"Hallelujah! He finally saw the light," Zee replied. "My guy takes walk-ins."

Fitz had no second thoughts as he sat down in the barber's chair.

"Hank, see if you can make him look almost as good as me. He's gettin' married today," Zee directed.

"You want to go that short with it?" Hank asked.

Fitz eyed Zee and said, "Maybe a little longer."

As Fitz faced the mirror, Hank fitted his clippers with a guard and proceeded to work over Fitz's beard. After the first pass, Fitz cringed.

"Sorry. Did it pull?" Hank asked.

"No, it's just a shock," Fitz replied.

"Imagine the shock on Katía's face when she sees you," Zee said.

"It might be a good idea to warn her," Ben added.

Hank finished trimming the beard and mustache and asked, "What about the hair?"

Fitz eyed his hair. "I hadn't realized how gray it was getting."

"You have a kind of Willie Nelson look," Hank said.

"Yeah. Maybe one step at a time. Just trim up the ends," Fitz added.

"I hope you're not planning to wear a cowboy hat," Zee teased.

"That's a great idea!" Fitz said as he rubbed his hand across his beard. He double-checked the mirror to assure himself it was really his face he was touching.

"No. Just, no," Ben said. "No cowboy hat."

With Fitz sheared, they headed to Ben's to get dressed. Fitz donned his tuxedo, then pulled his hair behind his ears, putting it in a ponytail. *Katía deserves better than me, but I'll give her the best I have. I hope she's not making a mistake. I hope I'm not making a mistake. No, it feels too right to be wrong. I have to quit doubting myself. This is the path I was meant to take.*

"Whoowee! You're lookin' good!" Zee said.

"You're looking mighty sharp yourself," Fitz returned.

Zee had rented a black suit for the occasion. "I do clean up good, don't I?"

Ben came out also dressed in a black suit. "Perfect timing. We should be at the park with twenty minutes to spare."

Ben parked away from the point by the lake where the ceremony would take place. A few people had already arrived, mostly members of Katía's church. A wave of sadness hit when Fitz realized that neither he nor Katía had any family members to be there. It was replaced by a warm joy. *Ben, Zee, and Luna are our family.*

Carlos pulled in with Brian, who approached and shook Fitz's hand. "Today's the big day! I haven't seen Katía this happy in a long time. You two are going to be good for each other."

"Thanks," Fitz replied. "I know she's good for me. I just hope I can return the gift."

Brian patted him on the shoulder. "You'd better," he teased. Fitz winced, but Brian didn't seem to notice. He continued, "I love the beauty of this setting, and those pots of pink and white flowers really set it off."

"We can't complain about the weather, either," Ben noted, eyeing the clear blue sky. The temperature had already reached the mid-fifties. The wake left by a passing boat shimmered in the sun.

"You did arrange for no boats to go by during the ceremony, right?" Ben directed to Zee.

"Oops, I knew I forgot somethin'," Zee replied.

More cars pulled in. Fitz checked his watch: 11:18 a.m. He began to wonder if the two special guests would show. *I wish I knew what kind of cars they drove.* As he searched, he spotted Luna's car approaching.

Fitz's heart leapt, and his mind shifted gears. *She's here!* Katía had managed to keep him from seeing her dress, but with the park venue being open, there was no way to remain hidden till the ceremony began.

Fitz hurried over and opened the door for her. Katía reached out her hand, and Fitz helped her out of the car. He stood there wide-eyed, mouth opened. Katía did a double take before rubbing her hand along his beard.

"My, don't you look dapper," she said.

Fitz rubbed his beard as well, the sight of his bride causing him to forget he had had it trimmed. He was still speechless.

"I'll take your expression to mean that you approve of my dress."

Fitz finally found his voice. "You're gorgeous!"

Emotions ping-ponged in his heart. The realization that he was getting married today clicked into place, and a warm glow radiated from the very center of his soul. "We're getting married today!"

Katía smiled. "I see that. I believe you're happy about it, too."

"I'm very happy," Fitz replied.

"OK, you two lovebirds, it's time to get into our positions," Ben prompted.

When Fitz was able to take his eyes off Katía, he was surprised at how many people had gathered. Brian had organized them so that there was a center aisle.

"Zee, I believe you're going to have to drag the groom into position," Ben said.

Zee took Fitz's arm. "Come on. You can't get married standin' here."

When Fitz and Zee were in position next to Brian, someone from Katía's church pushed the button to play the Wedding March. Ben walked Katía down the "aisle" and stood beside her till Brian asked, "Who gives this woman to be married to this man?"

"Her park pals do," Ben said before taking his place beside Zee. Luna and Shirley flanked Katía.

Brian led them through the service, announced that they were husband and wife, then said, "You may kiss the bride."

Fitz took Katía into his arms, held her tightly, and kissed her. Brian presented them as Fitz and Katía Fitzgerald. The music started, and Fitz and Katía walked back down the aisle formed by the crowd.

With Katía on his arm, Fitz noticed several faces he recognized as they walked. There were Sarge, Captain, and a group of his residentially-challenged friends. When he noticed Winslow Johnston, a shock surged through him. Lost in the wonder of the ceremony, he had totally forgotten about the pending arrests.

Once he and Katía were past the crowd, Fitz leaned in and whispered, "We have a surprise for you."

"Oh? What is it?"

"It wouldn't be a surprise if I told you, would it?"

Katía hugged his arm and kissed him on the cheek. "Then I'll just have to savor the suspense."

The music stopped, and Brian invited everyone to join them for lunch under the pavilion.

As people lined up where the caterers were prepared to serve, Fitz caught Deputy James' eye. She nodded and spoke into her radio. Two deputy cars drove into the park and blocked the road.

"Watch this," Fitz said, having just finished serving his plate.

They watched as the deputies approached Councilman Johnston and Mayor Thompson. "You're under arrest for burglary of a place of religious worship."

There was an audible gasp from the crowd.

"You mean they were both involved?" Katía asked.

"Yep. We caught 'em red-handed," Zee added.

"They just couldn't resist another chance to denigrate the unhoused community," Ben added.

"Now you can honeymoon in peace," Zee said.

A healthy buzz had set up amongst the wedding attendees. Shirley came up to Katía. "Do you know what that was about?"

"Yeah. It appears the councilman and mayor are behind the break-ins at the church."

"Break-ins! You mean there's more than one? You mean our own member robbed us of the shelter collection? I ain't never!" Shirley bustled off to spread the news.

"Do you think they'll be able to prove they're behind Harley and Nate's crimes?" Katía asked.

"I bet that laundromat guy'll be the first to squeal," Zee said. "He'll be beggin' for a deal."

Ben laughed. "I bet you're right."

The entire crowd gawked as the deputies read Johnston and Thompson their Miranda rights. As they loaded them into the cars, Johnston gave Katía an evil look, then smiled.

"Hang on a minute." Katía set her plate down, walked over, and put her arm around Stacey Johnston. "I'm so sorry, Stacey."

"What am I going to do without him around?"

"We're going to help hold you up and help you take it one day at a time."

A tear rolled down Stacey's cheek when she turned and said, "Thank you. I'm going to need some help getting through this. I disagreed with the stance he took against unhoused people, but I never thought he'd do anything like steal from his own church. The mayor put a lot of pressure on him to get rid of the unhoused but wanted Winslow to be the one taking the lead on the project. I can't believe he took it that far."

Katía squeezed her into a hug and held back telling her about the other charges that would probably soon be added. She patted her on the shoulder and returned to the table where Fitz had just sat down.

"Let's try to forget about the drama and enjoy the reception," Luna suggested.

CHAPTER 39

The smiles and laughter usually associated with a wedding reception soon replaced the buzz over the arrests. People milled about near the pavilion while the last to get their plates finished eating.

Fitz noticed he was getting nervous but couldn't figure out why.

"You've gotten mighty quiet," Katía observed. "What's up?"

"I'm not sure," Fitz replied. "I'm just …"

"It's too late to get cold feet," Zee said. "The knot is tied!"

"It's not that," Fitz said. "I'm totally in love with this lady and am happy to be married to her. I can't put my finger on what's bugging me."

"It's not the look Johnston gave Katía, is it?" Ben asked. "That was pure evil."

"That could be it," Fitz said. "You don't think they could have another salvo planned, do you?"

"The quicker we get you out of here, the less chance they'll have," Ben replied.

"I'm not rushing off from my reception just because he leered at me. I intend to enjoy myself and expect all of you to do the same," Katía protested. "Now let's mingle and enjoy this time."

A tap on her shoulder prompted Katía to turn.

"Surprise!" Luna said.

Confusion was replaced with recognition when Katía realized Laurie Jones and her mother, Jenny, were reaching to hug her.

Katía hugged them back and said, "Wow! I'm so happy to see you!"

"I'm so happy for you," Laurie, one of the teens whom the Inmanson boys had kidnapped last summer, gushed.

Right behind Laurie and Jenny came Victoria Lopez and her family. Victoria had been abducted and threatened with her life after refusing to steal opioids for her boss. Katía hugged them all, saying, "I'm glad you came. How are you doing?"

"We had to come when Luna told us about the wedding," Victoria said.

"I'm happy you made it," Katía added as she hugged Sophia, Victoria's daughter.

Looking over Sophia's shoulder, Katía saw Joseph standing next to Zee.

"You can thank me for roundin' this one up," Zee said.

"Hey, Joseph! Thanks for coming," Katía said, coming to hug the man who had been caught up in Dr. Max Herringer's evil scheme to experiment on people last winter.

Fitz joined in the hugs, struggling to lift his sore arms and hoping no one would pat his back on the aching band left by the 2x4.

Wiping the two tears that escaped her eyes, Katía said, "I'm touched that you got everybody together, Luna. This makes today even more special."

After chatting with that group for a while, Katía grabbed Fitz's hand and pulled him over to talk with a group of her church members.

Sheriff Tucker tapped Fitz on the shoulder. "Congratulations, Fitz! I'm happy for you."

"Thank you, Sheriff. I can't believe I'm so fortunate to have this lady as my wife."

"I want you to know that I'd be happy to have you back on the force, even if it's just part-time. We could use a good man like you."

"I don't know what to say," Fitz replied.

"Just think about it and let me know sometime after your honeymoon."

"I'll do that," Fitz said, even more joy filling his heart.

"It looks like Katía was right to stay and enjoy the reception," Ben said. "Nobody in their right mind would attack with this many people around, anyway."

"True, but they might not be in their right minds," Zee replied.

"Johnston probably thought they were off the hook for a while since Katía and Fitz would be gone on their honeymoon. I bet he thought no one would discover the robbery till Sunday morning," Luna added. "I don't think there's anything to worry about. Let's mingle!"

Luna pulled Carlos along to visit with a few friends and to meet some of the folks they didn't know.

Zee started toward Fitz and Katía, but Ben caught his arm.

"I've been thinking, Zee," he said. "I'd be honored to have you as a houseguest on a permanent basis."

"You askin' me to marry you?" Zee grinned.

"Goofball, I'm asking if you'd like to live with me."

"I come with a bit of drinking, you know."

"I know. I'll even join you on special occasions."

Zee studied Ben's eyes. "Me and King'll think about it, but I'm inclined to say yes."

"I hope you will," Ben said. He and Zee joined Fitz and Katía.

Katía waved Brian over. "This is Brian," she said, introducing him to the group of church members. "He'll be filling in for me this Sunday."

"We're looking forward to hearing you preach," Shirley said.

"I'm looking forward to sharing the day with you," Brian replied.

Fitz was trying to pay attention to the conversation while keeping an eye on the road leading into the park. Even though the assurances the others had given made sense, he was still uneasy.

After Katía had made the rounds and introduced Fitz to more people than he would ever be able to remember, she looked him in the eyes. "Are you ready to go?"

The act of leaving the park hit Fitz with a sense of certainty. "We're married," he replied.

"Yes, indeed," Katía grinned, kissing him.

With her kiss, the worry melted away, replaced by the warm glow of joy. "Let's get going," he said.

Luna directed Ben, Zee, Carlos, and a few others to load the gifts and cards into Katía's car. Next, she arranged the crowd into two lines while Ben, Zee, Brian, and Carlos distributed packets of birdseed.

Katía and Fitz gathered Ben, Zee, and Luna. "You are the best friends anyone could ever have," Katía said. "Thank you for all you've done to make this day so special."

"Ditto," Fitz added. He knelt down to pet Buffett. "Ben and Zee are going to take care of you for a few days. I'll see you when we get back. It's going to be OK."

"Meow."

Fitz handed Ben the leash.

The crowd cheered and tossed seeds as Fitz and Katía walked to the car. When they got to Katía's Prius, they stopped, waved, and brushed birdseed off each other before hopping in.

Katía put the Prius in drive, then reached over and took Fitz's hand. "I'm so happy to be married to you."

Fitz kissed the back of her hand. "Same here."

"If we can change in a hurry, we should be at St. Simons by nine," she added. "I hope you don't mind driving. I'm beat. What do you want to do for supper?"

"I'll be happy to drive, but don't know exactly what I want for supper. Just something simple after that big lunch."

"But you didn't eat much."

"Still, I'd rather get to the rental house than spend a long time eating."

"I see," Katía grinned. "Me, too."

Ever vigilant, Fitz noticed a red pickup truck pull out from a parking spot near the boat ramp area of the park. He watched as it made its way down the hill and toward the exit. Katía got to the stop sign and pulled out ahead of the vehicle. Fitz tensed up. *Surely they're not following us.*

When Katía turned onto Cleveland Highway, he tried to bend and look out the side mirror without her noticing. She noticed.

"What's wrong?" Katía asked.

"That red pickup left the park when we did and is still behind us."

"Relax, Fitz. It's over. The two bad guys are in custody."

"Yeah, but their minions aren't … and the laundromat guy isn't. We might have irked him with our visits."

A Georgia State Patrol office was located up the road about a mile. Fitz directed Katía to turn into it. She did, and the pickup kept going.

"See, they weren't after us," Katía said. "Let's go honeymoon and let all of this stress melt away."

Fitz wasn't assured but squeezed her hand and said, "To St. Simons!"

Katía punched in the code to unlock the door to her house and stepped back. "Should you carry me over the threshold? … No, not a good idea. We might pull your … whooo!"

Fitz scooped her up and carried her inside. "Now it's official."

After a long kiss, Katía pulled back. "Just a few more hours. Let's get changed and hit the road." She gave him a wink and headed to the bedroom. "Don't just stand there!"

Fitz set his Beretta on a table and noticed something seemed different. It took a moment to figure out what it was: a new cat bed sat next to Cotton's and Snow's beds.

"You got Buffett a bed," he said, touched by the gesture.

"Surprise!" she said, returning to where he stood.

"So that's what you were talking about that hadn't arrived yet."

"That's it. Now, come on so we can get going."

He followed her down the hall and turned into the room where he had been keeping his clothes.

"Not in there, silly. I have your clothes laid out in here. We're married now, you know."

As he entered Katía's bedroom, she turned around. "I need some help unzipping."

Fitz eyed the top of the dress where there was a clasp. After three tries, the clasp came open, and he pulled down the zipper.

"Thanks," she said and gave him a quick kiss. "Now get changed so we can get on our way."

Fitz doffed his tuxedo and, struggling to take his eyes off Katía, managed to put on the new outfit she had bought him for the honeymoon.

The sound of a vehicle drew his attention. Hurrying to the living room, he looked out the window to see the same red pickup in the driveway.

"We have company," he called. "Dial 911, then get your gun ready."

Fitz watched as four men got out of the truck. "Looks like they're serious this time. There's four of them. The driver is the creep from the laundromat." He stepped away from the window, the one that had just been repaired after the rock had broken it. He was grateful Ben had managed to arrange the repair in the midst of all the chaos of the last week and hoped it wasn't about to be broken again.

Katía hurried up to Fitz, still talking to the 911 operator and holding her Glock. "It looks like two of them are going around back. … No, there goes a third one."

The man from the laundromat stayed in front of the house, holding a baseball bat.

"They're going to break in from the back. This guy's watching to make sure we don't run out the front," Fitz said. "Keep an eye on him."

Fitz moved to the back door, trying to decide whether to start shooting through the window or wait until they tried to come in.

"The 911 lady wants us to go to an interior room and hide," Katía called to Fitz.

"Tell her we're armed, and that's the last thing I intend to do. We plan to defend ourselves." *Now, let's see how this plays out.*

CHAPTER 40

Fitz crouched behind the couch and waited. He heard one of the men test the door to find it was locked. Expecting them to try busting down the door, he was surprised when he heard the tell-tale sound of someone picking the lock. *My estimation of these goons just went up a notch.*

When the locks were opened, Fitz heard a whistle. He readied himself, trusting Katía would figure out what the whistle meant.

The back door flew open, but nobody was there. *I know what that means.* Fitz waited, his gun aimed at the empty doorway. A head appeared and pulled back. Fitz exercised patience, holding his fire until one of the men stepped into the doorway.

Then it happened. The first man stepped full into the doorway, and Fitz fired, knocking him backward with the blast. *Now, what will they do?*

"We were going to just beat you up a bit, teach you a lesson, but now you're gonna pay with your lives," one of the men yelled.

Not wanting to give away his position, Fitz remained silent. He spotted Katía and put a finger to his lips. She nodded, turning her attention back to the front.

Out of habit, Fitz made a mental note that he had fourteen rounds left. He waited and watched, wondering if another guy would try entering. Noticing movement in the distance, he realized what was coming. He moved to the side of the room in order to be safe from the cover-fire that was about to hit.

Sure enough, four shots fired, followed by goon number two jumping through the doorway. Fitz fired, hitting him in the chest to the right of the heart. The man spun onto the floor, then crawled back out the door.

Fitz heard Katía say, "Make that two ambulances." He wondered if the third man would give it a try. He didn't have ling to wait.

The man came full speed through the door, jumping, rolling, and coming to a knee, ready to fire. Before he could locate Fitz in the dimly-lit room, Fitz fired, hitting him in the shoulder. The man spun backward, landing on his face. Fitz was up and planted a foot on his back.

"Drop the weapon, or the next round goes through your head."

"No, make that three ambulances," Fitz heard Katía say.

Scooping up the gun, Fitz called to Katía, "What's the man in the front doing?"

"Moving toward the back," she replied.

"'They don't give up, do they?" Fitz said, moving back into position to the side of the door.

"Wait, apparently he changed his mind. He's hightailing it toward the truck."

Fitz stayed in position but noticed Katía aiming her phone out the window. *Good idea.* When he heard the truck crank up, Fitz poked his head out the back door. Both men were groaning and writhing in pain. The third one remained on the den floor.

"Are they dead?" Fitz heard Katía call.

"No, but I can remedy that if you like." He presented the men with his most menacing smile. He scooped up the two handguns they had dropped outside.

"I'm going to keep an eye on these three. Maybe they'll give me another reason to shoot them," Fitz called to Katía.

She appeared in the doorway. "You got blood on my carpet."

Fitz was flummoxed.

"That seems like a good enough reason to shoot," she added.

Fitz laughed as the sound of sirens filled the air.

The deputies frisked the three men, and the paramedics loaded them into the ambulances and drove away.

Deputy James approached Fitz and Katía. "You sure have an odd way of honeymooning," she said with a smile.

"About that. How soon can we get out of here?" Katía asked.

"We need to process the scene and have you answer a few questions, then you're free to go. I'll try to make it quick."

With the interviews concluded and evidence collected, Diann added, "Now go on and have a wonderful honeymoon."

"You don't have to tell us twice!" Katía said.

"What in the world are you doing?" Deputy James asked when she noticed Fitz kneeling on the floor.

"I'm going to try to clean up the mess I made."

Katía and Deputy James laughed, and Deputy James said, "Get up from there and let me handle that. Y'all finish packing or whatever else you have to do."

Fitz surrendered the scrub brush and said, "Thanks. I don't want to start the marriage off in trouble."

Finally loaded into the car, Fitz turned onto the road and headed toward St. Simons.

"We're only an hour and a half late. That's not too bad," Katía said. "We can make up some of that by eating in the car."

"I'm going to miss Buffett."

"Not as much as you think you will," Katía grinned. "I'll make sure of that."

A NOTE FROM THE AUTHOR

Thank you so much for investing your time in reading **Two Stolen Men!** I trust you enjoyed the novel and hope you had a chance to read the prior books in the series: **The Hidden Scalpel, The Missing Pill, and The Dying Cave.**

Each review or rating my books receive means a lot to me. I would be grateful if you would take the time to write a brief review or leave a star rating on the site from which you purchased the book. Your input helps other readers know if my books are right for them.

If you enjoy my writing and would like to get notified of new releases and receive humorous articles and book recommendations, please sign up for my newsletter on the website: www.dwainwrites.com. Along with your newsletter sign-up, you get a free eBook that tells the story of Fitz's life during the time he met Sharon. On the website, you can also learn more about me and my other books.

Keep reading, and may life be gentle and joyful!
Dwain

ACKNOWLEDGEMENTS

With each book I write, I become more convinced that it cannot be done without help. I am amazed at the generosity of the people who have helped with the creation of **Two Stolen Men.** B. J. Myers-Bradley was willing to read through the manuscript and provide feedback to make this a better story. I truly appreciate his time and insights. Clara Bella Rose, a fellow author, provided her authorly insights to improve the manuscript and her artistic eye to improve the cover.

Merilyn Guerry served as the book's editor and never ceases to amaze me with her skills at hunting down and exposing the grammatical glitches hiding in a manuscript.

I am grateful for the artistic skills of Becky Franks for the author photo and to Getcovers for the cover.

Writing is one of my joys in life, and I thank each person who helped me bring that joy to fruition in the form of **Two Stolen Men!**

BOOKS BY DWAIN CASSADY

THE PARK PALS SERIES:
THE HIDDEN SCALPEL
THE MISSING PILL
THE DYING CAVE
TWO STOLEN MEN

THE DARK WINGS TRILOGY:
DARK WINGS RISING
DARK WINGS DARING
DARK WINGS SOARING

THE WILLOW NOVELS:
FEATHERS IN WATER
FEATHERS IN FLIGHT

ADVENT DEVOTIONALS:
INSIGHTS FROM MATTHEW
PRESENCE IN THE MANGER
THE COMING LIGHT
THE SOIL OF SALVATION